Falling Leaves

Falling Leaves

ALLEGORIES, FABLES, AND PARABLES FROM THE TREE OF LIFE

M. C. REITZ

*Falling Leaves: Allegories, Fables, and Parables
from the Tree of Life*

By M.C. Reitz

ISBN 978-602-8397-11-7

Printed in the United States

In autumn, colorful red, gold, yellow, orange and brown falling leaves, having nourished the tree, enrich the soil and become compost for new life; so too my experiences, the compost of my life, have nourished me. These allegories, fables and parables fall from me with the trust that they may nourish you.

Contents

Acknowledgements

In my first book, *Dawn-light*, I thanked every one in general who helped me along my path. With *Falling Leaves* I would like to thank folks who had to live with this man who tried to be quite rational and yet who had stories to be told that came from another place in him. I am grateful for my children (Aaron, David, Matthew, Jessica and Rachel), their mother (Jeanne Christie Reitz), my brother, my sisters and my closest friends.

I give special thanks to my partner, Janis Billings, for encouraging me to publish my writing and her many hours of typing and editing for me, as well as her sister Nancy Nelson who did the final editing.

Of course, thanks to Beverly Chapman who co-wrote three of these stories. We wrote by e-mail with neither knowing where the story was headed as we passed text to one another. There was no consultation on what would happen next. We simply added to what the other wrote till it was obvious that the story was over.

Finally, thanks to Mark Hanusz, good friend and owner of Equinox Publishing, for creating a beautiful package for my stories.

The Wisdom of the Mule

A man owned three mules. They were the means to his livelihood. At daybreak each day, he placed large sacks over their backs; the sacks reached down on both sides as low as their belly bottoms. With a light stick and strong commands he herded the mules along the mountain paths to the stone quarry, loaded them with blocks of stone and plodded back along the paths to where people were building. Sometimes he loaded them with gravel, sand or whatever was needed.

The man was not rich but he earned enough money to feed himself, his wife and his two children. They had good, if not fancy, clothes to wear and there was always a little extra money for the fair or other entertainments. All in all, he was a good hard-working man who provided all the necessities for his family.

One extremely hot day with the sun's withering heat drenching the man in sweat and the mouths of the mules lathered with foam as he urged them up the steep mountain trail with heavy loads, the man was suddenly struck by the suffering of his mules. He felt sorry for them. He thought to himself that on the next day he would not fill their bags so full.

On the next day, even though the man had lightened the load on his mules, he continued to feel sad for them. Therefore, on the following day, he made their loads even lighter. He also took some money that was saved for his family's entertainment in order to buy special grain to feed the mules. Each day he felt more and more sorry for the mules, lightened their load even more and fed them more grain. As time went on, the mules became lazy and obstinate. Within the month, the mules were working only one day a week and carried very little on that day. Meanwhile, the man's family suffered in silence. They dared not speak. After all, he was the husband, the father, and no one should question him lest they show disrespect. Once his wife tried to tell him that they had too little to eat. The man flew into a rage. He scolded her shouting, "Have you no pity on the beasts of burden? Quit your complaining."

Meanwhile, the mules grew huge with fat and no longer worked. The man did not feel his own hunger and he was blind to the plight of his family who suffered in silence.

One night Death came to the poor man's door. She had come for the youngest child, the man's only son. The man was awake and saw death enter. "Wait," he cried, "Why are you here?" Death responded, "Your son has suffered enough. I come to help him to his next life." The man cried out, "Please, no! Don't kill my son!" Death responded, "I do not kill. You sow the seeds of your own destruction and the destruction of one another. You have killed your own son. I am merely here to make his transition easy." Death walked over to the small boy who was breathing his last. Death embraced the boy and disappeared, leaving the boy's lifeless body behind.

The father wept bitterly as his son's body burned on the funeral pyre. His wife would not speak to him and his only remaining child was weak and frail. He wailed, "I have killed my son. I am killing my family. Oh, my karma must have been so bad in my past life. What will my next life be like?"

The man went out to the tethered mules saying to himself, "These poor beasts of burden, I must release them from their duty so that they can freely roam these hills, free from man's work."

Before he could release the first mule, the mule spoke, "Do not release me. I shall have to forage for my food and I shall grow thin. I may starve to death or be too weak to run from the tiger, which wishes to feed on me. Please take care of me." The man did not release him.

The man went to the second mule and it spoke to him, as did the first. The man did not release him either.

On approach to the third mule, the man noticed that it was not nearly as fat as the first two. In fact, the third mule looked fit enough to work. He asked, "Why are you not like the other two?"

"Master," said the mule, "My nature is to work. My body feels good when I have useful things to do. When you fed us extra grain I ate little. When you did not lead us to work I exercised on my own. I have kept myself prepared for the day when you would again give me the gift of useful work. Please, master, do not release me. Give me work!"

The man looked at the mules and looked at his home with his suffering family within. He had turned good animals into useless ones. He had killed his only son and brought great suffering to his family. He sat down and wept. He decided he must throw himself off the mountaintop. His sins were too much for him to live with.

As the man wept, the third mule came up close to him and nuzzled his neck and ear. The man felt kindness and compassion from the mule. The mule quietly pleaded, "Please master, for my own good, for your own good, for the good of your family give me a task. It is my nature to serve. Please master, you are a good man. Together we can build a new life for you and your family. Please!"

The man stood up and hugged the mule. Then he looked at the other mules. "What about them?" he asked.

The mule replied, "Oh, they were perfectly happy before you began indulging them. Your indulgence has created the seed of their destruction. However, there is yet time. It will take effort on your part. They will work again and become fit. They will again enjoy the purpose for which they were made."

The man thanked the mule and hugged him. He assured the mule that life would be good again. The very next day he placed the sacks on the backs of his mules and herded them to the quarry, much to the surprise of the two fat lazy mules and his wife. At first the mules balked at the work. Eventually they felt new strength and vitality in their bodies. They again enjoyed the feeling of doing useful work. They were tired at the end of the day but they never slept so well and woke up fresh every morning. Likewise the man slept well, woke up fresh, breathed deeply of the mountain air, and welcomed the sun, the rain, the clouds or whatever nature brought him. The man, the mules and the man's family led a full good life. The family was never rich and the mules were never asked to work quite as hard as they had before the man's indulgence. The man's wife gifted him with two more sons and a daughter. If not wealthy, they were rich in love and lived well enough.

Great Grandfather Rock

The young boy overheard his grandfather speaking to his mother.

> *Moon-spirit wanes.*
> *Great Grandfather Rock waits.*
> *The sand gently shifts*
> *as Wind-spirits whisper;*
> *'Who comes here to save my people?*
> *Great Grandfather Rock waits.*

Grandfather was very old and spoke strange poems and yet the boy's mother always listened intently.

Grandfather fell asleep, mother sat down to stitch together a deerskin pouch, father was gone for a week hunting with the other men and baby sister was playing contentedly with some small stones. The silence, the warmth and glow of the fire at the center of the pit house made for a warm, peaceful, contented feeling.

The boy sat on the clay floor close to his mother and asked, "What did grandfather mean by that poem?"

The boy knew by his mother's silence and confused expression that she was not sure of what to say.

Finally, being very careful with her words Mother spoke, "Oh, you know grandfather; he is always saying strange things."

The boy knew by the sound of his mother's voice and her strange look that she was not telling him what she knew. There was something very important in grandfather's words.

The next day the boy again overheard his mother and grandfather speaking in soft voices.

Grandfather spoke with great agitation, "Someone must find Great-Grandfather Rock or we will suffer greatly."

His mother replied with heavy sadness, "Yes, without rain the seeds will not grow and the animals stray far away. Many of us will die. My husband says that we may have to move the village. If we move into a space held by others there will be fighting. What can that dream have to do with it?"

"I do not know," said grandfather, "In my dream, the boy found Great-Grandfather Rock and our world was once again in harmony. We had all we needed."

"Where is this rock?" asked mother.

"I don't know!" answered grandfather.

"It was just a dream," said mother. "Some dreams show us the way and others deceive...I do not know...."

"Many of us will die soon," said grandfather. "Send the boy now!"

"Where am I to send him," said mother, "...to nowhere? What direction? How far? What does the rock look like? Why him? He is so young. Father, you must dream some other dream."

Hearing all this, the boy became frightened for himself, his family and the whole village.

He thought, "Were they all to die? What did Grandfather mean when he said that in his dream the boy found Great-Grandfather Rock? Was he that boy? Grandfather had told his mother to send him out. His mother told grandfather to dream a new dream. Did this mean that she did not believe the dream to be true?"

The boy, scared and confused, ran down to the dry wash to pretend he was a bush along its banks and sit in silence.

The boy's name was Pale Moon because he was born on a cloudy night with only a sliver of waning Moon-Spirit. The boy remembered his grandfather's poem and the words "Moon-Spirit wanes." In a deep silence surrounded by the stillness of the dry wash, Pale Moon became convinced that he must follow his grandfather's dream to save his people. Yet, where should he go? In what direction and exactly what should he look for? His mother and grandfather did not seem to have any answers.

As he sat alone, Pale Moon became less frightened and more determined. The gentle Night-Air Spirits whispered from the South at this time of year. He would walk into the whisper until he found Great-Grandfather Rock. He would travel in a direction his people had not traveled. His father and the other men always hunted to the North because it was believed there was nothing except heat and death to the South.

That night when everyone was asleep, Pale Moon rolled up his sheepskin and filled a deerskin pouch with ground seed and dried rabbit meat. He quietly left the village and walked into the whispering wind. He traveled for seven turns of the Great Sun-Spirit, eating only small portions of his provisions and sucking the juice of cactus apples that he gathered along the way. The days were hot and dry, the nights bone-chilling cold.

On the seventh day, Pale Moon from a long distance could see a single huge rock rising out of the flat land. It stood totally alone, as did Pale Moon. As he approached, the red smooth rock towered over Pale Moon.

"Could this be the rock?" thought Pale Moon. "There is nothing here. No water or game to help my people."

Tired and discouraged, Pale Moon sat down in the shade of the rock and began to weep. When he had no more tears he sucked the juice from his last cactus apple and fell asleep. He awoke in the middle of the night, covered himself with his sheepskin and curled up close to the rock, which had absorbed the Great Sun- Spirit's heat. He felt as if he were curled up close to his own mother's warm body.

Pale Moon dreamed the story he had been told since he was an infant and which was acted out by the dancers at ceremonies. The people came into this world through the will of Mother Earth. Father Sky called them forth. In his dream he watched the people emerge from a hole in the earth. They raised their heads to Father Sky and shouted for joy. All the animals and plants came up from that hole and took their places on the earth. Life was abundant for all living beings.

Pale Moon awoke as the first arms of Great Sun-Spirit streaked across the sky. He felt peaceful and content nestled in the arms of the great rock. From Mother Earth his people had come and to Mother Earth they would return. Is that not the chant they sang when someone's Spirit had gone to join Father Sky?

Suddenly, Pale Moon stood. Far in the distance across the flat land was a jagged black line. Without much thought, Pale Moon began to walk towards that black mark. As the Great Sun-Spirit drew higher in Father Sky and as he approached closer to where he thought the black mark had been, it disappeared. Pale Moon continued to walk. He walked for almost one half of the day before he realized that his body was shivering in the heat and his legs wanted to collapse under him. Yet, he kept going.

The Great Sun-Spirit was at its highest peak when Pale Moon suddenly stopped. He could go no further. It was not the heat, the fatigue or the thirst that stopped him. He could go no further because he was on a precipice looking down into a deep canyon. A stream of water ran through the canyon and deer grazed in tall grass. Mountain sheep scampered among the rocks.

Pale Moon's first thought was that this was the place from which all people, plants and animals emerged.

He scouted the rim of the canyon and found a place where he could begin his climb down. Along the way he found a pool of water in a crevice of rock. He also found berries and other edible vegetation. He climbed down, down, down into the canyon. As he reached the bottom, darkness had begun to set in. It was much warmer in the canyon and the heated rocks gave him comfort as he found a rock shelf on which to sleep.

Pale Moon dreamed that his people would come to this place and build homes safely up on rock ledges above the canyon floor. They would be safe from above and below, as the canyon would provide for all their needs.

Upon returning home, having been gone for nearly fourteen turns of the Great Sun-Spirit, the village stared at him in disbelief. The story of what he had found brought great joy among his people and plans were made to move the village to the canyon. They built their homes on the canyon walls as Pale Moon had foreseen. The canyon brought them abundance for many generations.

Great-Grandfather Rock became a place of pilgrimage for Pale Moon's people. When troubles came and decisions were to be made, they would sit in silence like a bush near Great-Grandfather Rock and wait for him to speak to their hearts. They say he never failed to answer them.

(Every child will take a journey [a long walk] to save his or her people. Growing up is not easy and every child will reach the point where he or she must understand that it is their turn to take responsibility for the people.

Every person must find their Great-Grandfather Rock by which to sit silently like a bush and meditate on what to do next for the good of the people.... written for Journey Morales.)

Jack's Grandpa

My grandpa is young!

My grandpa exercises and eats healthy food.

My grandpa does not work.

He travels to far away places.

He says that he helps people and does not ask for money.

He works for the fun of it; he volunteers!

I asked grandpa, "When will you go to Indonesia again?"

Grandpa was surprised I asked the question.

Grandpa said, "I don't know, Jack. Why do you ask?"

I told him, "Grandpa, when you go far away, you come back with interesting stories and new things."

My grandpa is like a Jack-in-the-box.

Oops, don't get confused; I'm Jack and he is grandpa.

Like a Jack-in-the-box, now you see him and now you don't.

Grandpa is always a surprise.

He surprised me one day when he cut off his long hair and shaved his beard.

He looked like a new grandpa.

When he goes away for a long time and then comes back, I still know him no matter what he looks like. He is my grandpa.

Grandpa Goes to India

We live on a big round ball called earth.

Grandpa took an airplane to the other side of the ball. He went to a place called India.

When he got on the plane he noticed the women who took care of the passengers dressed very differently than us. They wore something called a sari. I'll have to find a picture to see what that is.

Instead of saying "Hello" or "Good morning," the flight attendants said "Namaste." In our words, grandpa said, "Namaste means my spirit greets your spirit."

I asked grandpa, "What does spirit mean?"

Grandpa said, "Spirit, Jack, is the real you, deep inside, that can think about and love everything. Even though I am an old man, at one time I was a baby. My body changed but my spirit is the same spirit. When my body is too old, Jack, just like those wilted flowers; it will stop and dry up. Yet, Jack, my spirit lives without my body."

I did not understand what grandpa said; I have to think about it.

Maybe when I am as old as him, I'll understand.

On the airplane grandpa ate rice and vegetables that tasted very different from what I eat. It had something in it called curry.

When grandpa got off the airplane in India, he went to the bathroom. When he went into the toilet stall, there was no toilet. There was a hole in the floor and painted marks showing where to put your feet. That was interesting.

When grandpa tried to cross the street, he saw sights he had never seen before.

Elephants were walking down the middle of the street, and cows too.

The streets were filled with small cars, motorbikes, three-wheeled taxis and animals rushing forward without stopping, just like a big river.

Crowds of people moved along the sidewalks. Women carried on their heads large loads of fruits, vegetables, firewood, bricks, eggs, chickens in baskets and almost anything else you can imagine.

Grandpa saw rich people and very poor people. Mainly, he saw lots of people.

Grandpa saw happy little children who yelled at him, "Dadaji, dadaji, dadaji." That means "Grandpa, grandpa, grandpa." Grandpa likes hearing them say that and it reminded him of me.

Grandpa went to a place where Indian people pray.

A man took him to the front where there were beautiful statues.

A young boy poured water into the man's hands. The man sipped some of the water and then splashed the rest on his head.

Grandpa did the same.

The young boy then painted a yellow mark on the man's head and did the same for grandpa.

The man had to go and grandpa sat there for a long time. He was happy to be there.

Grandpa went to a place where men were locked up because they had problems.

Grandpa tried to help the men with their problems.

When the men met grandpa they tried to bow down to him and touch his feet like he was someone very important.

Grandpa gave them a big hug and a smile before they could bow down.

Grandpa wanted them to know that he liked them and that they were very important.

Someone was trying to get the children to sing and dance.

They were scared.

Grandpa jumped up and did a silly dance and sang a silly song.

All the children laughed.

All the children began to sing and dance.

Every day grandpa passed people who were making a building.

They had no machines and worked very hard doing everything by the strength of their bodies, hands, arms and legs.

When grandpa passed by, these beautiful people would stop their work and laugh and talk with him. Grandpa did not understand their language; it did not matter, grandpa had a good time.

Everyday grandpa watched men and mules go up and down the rocky paths carrying heavy loads.

Everyday he watched families with small children walk down the mountain to find work to make some money to live. In the darkness at night they came up the mountain to their small shacks. They had no bathroom, no water except what they carried from the well, and made their fire to cook with from dried cow poop.

Grandpa said all the people he met in India were very nice people. When he met people on the paths they bowed, folded their hands and said Namasté.

Now, if you do not watch too much TV, do your homework, and play outside, tomorrow I'll tell you the story of grandpa in Haiti.

Griz and Bee

Grizzly bears do not know each other by name. They know each other by scent or sight or sound...soooooooo the grizzly of our story has no name; yet, for the sake of the story we will call him "Griz."

Griz grew like all the other young bears: fighting, tumbling, racing, digging roots, gobbling a mouth full of berries and nuts and eventually hunting and killing. All the bears especially liked salmon.

Our Griz however had a soft spot in his personality that did not allow him to enjoy the aggressive part of the life of a bear, especially the killing and eating of flesh. He preferred berries and roots and nuts and especially honey. He was in ecstasy when he slurped honey and he would lick a spot for hours where honey had been.

Griz tried to play the rough games all the other bears his age played. He was big enough, strong enough, and yet did not have the aggressive attitude of the others. Eventually the others recognized his soft spot. They did not tease him; they simply left him alone to create his own day-dreamy world.

One beautiful day in late summer the bears were tearing apart a rotted tree trunk to get at the honey stored inside by a swarm of bees. The bees were furious and attacked the bears without any effect. Even though honey was Griz's favorite food he was uncomfortable participating in the violence. He usually only ate the remnants of the honey after the fighting was done and the bees and bears had left the scene. On this day as he sat aside he noticed a bee circling his head. It did not attack and simply came to rest on his head. It seemed like the bee did not wish to participate in the fighting either. Griz had the desire to know more about this little bee.

"Hello Mr. Bear" said Bee.

"Grrrizzz" said Griz.

"Griz, may I rest on your head today?

"Wow, I love the view of the world from the top of your head, where I can stop and not be so terribly busy for a while. Why do bees think they have to work so hard and be so busy all day? Don't they see that they are missing the aroma and beauty of the flowers they visit? Other bees never stop to watch the clouds floating by. They do not stop to visit with me and share their adventures. Their lives are all about work but there is so much more.

"And bees get so angry, what is the point of that? You will eat our honey whether I stab you with my stinger or not, and I would lose my stinger. I would lose the time that I could use instead to make a new honeycomb, or collect pollen, or enjoy sitting on your head. And the energy, it would make me tired to get so angry. And when bees go back home they are often still angry, even when there is no bear to be angry with any longer.

"Oh Griz, why did God make me a bee? I am not very good at it...."

Griz pondered the little bee as it seemed to sing to him with its buzzing around his head. Griz was a little slow in his responses to other bears, much less this talkative little bee. Actually Griz had never talked to any creature except of his own kind and was a bit at a loss as to what to say. The little bee had been so open about her differences from other bees and her inability to fit in. Griz thought of his own problem of not being like the other bears. He realized that even though she was a bee and he a bear, they were very similar in their being odd within their communities. Both were lonely.

Griz's mouth dropped open and his eyes opened like saucers when he realized that he had the opportunity to talk to a bee...a bee that makes honey...his favorite food.... "Perhaps," he thought, "I can say something about honey."

"Well, hi there Ms. Bee, I love honey."

The bee immediately recoiled, gave him a stern look and said with great agitation, "Don't you think I know that. You bears come every year and destroy our store of honey. Do you think we go through all that work just for your pleasure? We need that honey too and we work very hard for it and many of us die trying to protect it" The little bee had never felt so angry and wondered why she was talking to this bear in the first place. Griz realized that he had made a big mistake.

"Hey Griz," said Bee, "I love sitting on your head and watching the world. If I make you some honey will you show me the world?"

"Ohhhhhhhh," thought Griz...."What is this all about? This fresh little bee wants to be my friend? Wants to see the world with me? Wants to give me honey? Whoa! Little bee, I hardly know you and just a second ago you were mad at me for being a bear that eats your honey and now you want to travel with me and give me honey? I am a bear and you are a bee. That just doesn't happen between bears and bees. What about your bee family?

You certainly think differently than any flying creature that I know. Are you crazy?"

"Relax, Griz," said Bee. "I do not want anything but to share your perspective and to live in peace. I may be crazy, but I am thinking out of the box. Our families need not be involved, but if your family likes honey too and my family likes to view the world in a new way, they may like the same arrangement. Your world and my world are quite different; we may have much to learn from each other."

"Hmm...I am a little slower thinker than you," said Griz. "I am not sure exactly what you mean when you say 'out of the box'...it may be like what I feel because I am not exactly like all the other bears. I like peace and sharing is good...hmm...I think you're suggesting that we ought to cooperate instead of fight...hmm. The only thing I know about cooperation is that berries grow every year and we gobble them up; salmon spawn every year and we eat them, and honey bees make honey every year and we take what we want. I think I know what you mean. It is a one-way path into the bear's mouth. What is in it for you? Probably would be no more killing, fighting or trampling if there was something in it for the berries, the salmon and the bees...I don't know what that would look like...."

"Dear Grizzz," she buzzed. "You could carry my family and me on your head to the finest wildflower patches. I hear that your nose can sniff out anything. We will build a new hive with a honey reserve just for you. You can still find your berries and salmon while we work, and you can have honey for dessert."

"Wow! Bee, you are a dreamer. All the bears think that I'm a dreamer; you are way beyond me. Bees make honey for themselves and protect it with their stingers, and bears take what they want and destroy whatever gets in their way. That is nature. What you are talking about is unnatural...I mean...I like what you say but I don't think bears or bees will ever change their nature. Even if it worked for a little while between you and me, sooner or later the other bears and bees will attack us for being unnatural and betraying our species. It's a good thing no bear or bee has discovered us talking to one another; we would already be in trouble."

"OK, fine, Griz...deny your own happiness because you are worried about what others think of you. Stay stuck in your violent world because you are afraid of change. Don't try anything new that may make waves. Hold on to your miserable existence. I do not call it trouble; I call it progress...."

"You sound angry, Bee. I'm sorry. I didn't mean to make you angry. I was trying to explain the realities of the risk. I am very confused. I don't want to be in a violent world. That is why I was sitting aside when the other bears were tearing up your hive. That is why I am talking with you now. Give me a little slack. Then again, if you are prone to this kind of vindictive anger, I should be wary of you. Your anger speaks to me of a bee who must have it her way and no one is allowed to challenge her; no discussion, your way or the highway. That is certainly no way to help me adjust to your radical idea and no better an attitude than me being scared."

"I am sorry Griz, I am not used to working with bears and I would like to learn how to work with you. Please give me your ideas on how we can work together in peace. We have so much to learn from each other. Life is amazing."

"Well, I am a simple guy, Bee, and although I am a bit different from other grizzlies I still have to deal with my

DNA. So, first off, I would like you to understand that I have the DNA of a bear as you do that of a bee. Second, I think we must believe in a way that we were not taught, trusting that despite our DNA we can speak our truth to one another and not be offended by what we say or how the other reacts. Maybe we can form some sort of cooperative relationship beyond our nature of bear and bee. It seems to me the fact that we can speak to one another gives some hope that we are connected in a way that is beyond our form as bear and bee. In fact, I can see now that we both rely on so much outside ourselves. All the things that grow because there is sun and rain and soil and who knows what else. I guess I am beginning to understand the basis by which we can work together. We are already interconnected whether we like it or not.... So...hmm...I'm still not sure how we can work this out in the face of all the other bears and bees whose DNA control them and cannot begin to think beyond their own bellies.... Oh...hey Bee...maybe these thoughts will help us in the direction we would like to go. I love your honey. I love talking with you. I love watching you dance from one flower to another. Despite our different species you might say that in some ways I love you...do you love me?"

"Yes Griz, I do love you. My DNA makes me a busy, driven little bee. When I sit on your soft, fuzzy head I feel time slow to a stop. I feel the sun and breeze on my face. I love to watch your strong legs run through the fields of flowers. I love to watch you fish in the river and munch merrily on large mouthfuls of berries. Your appetite for life excites me."

"Well, thank you my little Bee. I am beginning to feel more comfortable having you around. Perhaps that is the secret. We simply enjoy being together and do not think about how we will organize our relationship. We'll hang out together when we can and when you need to go back to the hive, you go; the same with me and my family. Actually, since I am a male, I am expected to live by myself as I become more grown. They will just think me precocious when I ramble off to be on my own...."

"I agree, Griz," buzzed Bee. "We can be together as we see fit. For today let's take off for an afternoon adventure. We can go up that mountain there and see what flowers and berries are to be found."

And so they took off together for their first of many little adventures. Griz climbed high up the steep mountainside until they reached a meadow full of flowers, many they had never seen before. There, on a craggy broken old tree sat an eagle. This eagle looked very wise and strong.

"Awwwwwwk," screeched the eagle with, despite his age, an extremely high pitch which hurt Griz's ears and scared Bee from her perch in Griz's hair.... She buzzed about, disoriented, for at least thirty seconds.

"Hey, you" growled Griz to the eagle. You didn't need to do that...we're not here to hurt you."

The eagle screeched back. "You could not hurt me if you tried...but you are a bear, an animal that eats flesh as I do...and this is my territory!. Oh! A bee! I am sorry. I didn't see you.... Are you this bear's friend? Since when do bears and bees hang out together?"

"Listen," said Griz. "First of all, I am practically a vegetarian and do not like killing and this bee doesn't like stinging. We have a lot in common despite what you know about bears and bees...so perhaps you can keep your screeches as well as your talons to yourself and be a friend."

"Oh! Ha, ha, ha.... Oh! Ha, ha.... Oh...ha...ha, ha, ha, ha, ha...."
The eagle could barely stop laughing and nearly fell off his perch.

"What are you laughing at?" says Griz.

The eagle responded with more laughter. "The two of you...ha...ha...ha and me...."

"Are you making fun of us?" says Bee.

"Oh no...ha, ha, ha...Oh no.... I am probably the only vegetarian eagle in existence and I have made many friends with the little animals around here...I protect them."

Totally amazed, Griz and Bee looked at one another and thought, "This is absolutely crazy."

Bee buzzed around the eagle to get a better look. "What is your name?" asked Bee.

"My name is Justice," said the eagle.

"Oh!" said Bee. "Maybe you know where my friend Griz here can find some berriezzzzz? His stomach has been growling since we left home this morning."

"Oh yes, there is a wonderful patch of huckleberries just above that ridge. I can show you where if you will follow me." Justice soared high into the sky, through the little puffy clouds, gliding around in circles, and finally coming down on a tall tree next to a clearing on the mountain's east face.

Griz followed, bounding through the rocky terrain with Bee hanging onto his ear. Griz's eyes were wide and his mouth smiling and dripping in anticipation of a fresh, ripe huckleberry patch.

"Whoa!" exclaimed Griz as he came to a screeching halt at the edge of the berry patch. A big black bear lifted its head from the middle of the patch with a mouthful of berries. "This is already someone else's patch, Griz said. I don't want to fight over it."

Justice again went into a fit of laughter and coughed out, "Oh no, you don't have to worry. This is my friend Comfort. She is peaceful and will share this patch with you." With that, Comfort looked at Griz, smiled and went back to munching. Griz kept an eye on Comfort as he nibbled on the edges of the patch. Suddenly a cold breeze sent a shiver through Griz. It reminded him that if the huckleberries are ripe winter would soon be on its way and he would need to find a place to hibernate. Then he thought of Bee...she must return to her hive before it sealed in for the winter. He looked around: Where was Bee?

"Ah," there was Bee, busy checking out a large patch of fading wildflowers. She buzzed from flower to flower, wondering how she could ever make honey here all by herself. She needed her family to help with the honey and the comb building. Even with Griz's help she could not make honey here. Sadly she looked at Griz and knew it was time to head home when he finished eating his fill of berries.

Griz ambled over to where Bee was darting about from deadhead to deadhead, anxious and frustrated with the feel of an early winter coming on. Griz sighed and gave a soft grunt, letting Bee know that he was ready to go back to the meadow where they first met. Bee nestled into the warm soft fur behind his left ear and Griz ambled off down through the thick forest. There was a sad expectation of their parting when they reached the meadow. He had seen a cave not far from where Justice nested. He would come back up this way to spend the winter in deep slumber and Bee would return to her hive...or so that is what he thought.

Bee was warmly curled up in the thick fur next to Griz's ear. She whispered to him, "Griz, I am worried about the cold winter winds that are coming soon. Do you think you could find a place to store my hive for the winter? So many of us might freeze and die; if we were warmer we might all live to see spring." Somehow Bee knew that Griz could help them, he was naturally so warm and fluffy, and surely he must know how to keep her warm this winter.

Now Griz was thinking as hard as a bear could think.... He liked Bee very much and enjoyed her companionship. He felt she sort of belonged with him nestled behind his left ear and whispering sweet ideas to him. He enjoyed watching her buzzzzzz among the flowers as he sat nearby lazily snacking on some berries. She was as quick and flighty as he was slow and cumbersome. Somehow they enjoyed that difference. Now, this idea of Bee's did not seem that far-fetched; he may be able to help her and her family. Then a strange and terrible thought crossed Griz's mind. He was three years old and expected to live till about thirty. How long was Bee's lifespan? It seemed to him that insects did not live very long, maybe not even a year, maybe not even a few months. Griz stopped, lay down, lounged on his side and closed his eyes. Bee wondered what was wrong.

"Bee, I have an important question to ask you. It is very hard for me to ask it and yet I need to know the truth. What is the life span of a bee? How long can you expect to live?"

"Griz, if I am protected I might live through this winter," sighed Bee. Griz did not need to think about this. With Bee at his ear, his thick furry legs ran straight to Bee's hive and lifted the wooden frame with the hive right off the ground and very carefully headed to the cave he had found and had hoped to have all for himself.

He did not get far, however, before he saw a farmer with a shotgun aimed at his head. The farmer screamed at him, "Halt! Put down that hive, you stupid bear." Griz stopped, and just as the farmer was ready to shoot, Bee stung him right on the nose. The farmer dropped his gun, and Griz ran at full speed with the hive into the woods and up the hill to his secret cave.

Griz quickly entered the cave and placed the hive on a rock shelf near the entrance. He turned and saw the black bear, Comfort, already occupying the cave. In no mood for niceties, formalities or understanding, Griz let out a great roar of anger that surprised even him. Comfort scrambled out of the cave without hesitation in fear of the great Griz. Sadness and a weary feeling overcame Griz as he retreated to a snug corner at the back of the cave.

Bee, having reattached herself to Griz's left ear, moaned faintly, but loudly enough for Griz to hear between his sighs.

"Bee, are you OK?" asked Griz.

"No, Griz, I stung the farmer to save your life and my stinger detached. I will die now."

"Ah, Bee.... Why did you have to do that? If the farmer shot me, he would have just put the hive back where it was and life would have gone for everyone just as it had for years...." (Sobbing) "I'm just a grizzly bear and don't

36

produce anything for anyone. You produce honey for the world. I'm not even a very good bear. You are so wonderful and kind. Why did you do that? You had many more months to live to be with your family (putting his head down between his great paws).... Why did you do it, Bee...? I'll miss you, Bee."

As Bee lay dying, Comfort listened at the mouth of the cave to Griz's sobs and despair. She thought that Griz must be a sweet, sensitive bear and not the fierce, stupid bear he appeared to be. Comfort knew that Justice had led him to her valley and Justice was a very smart eagle indeed. She reentered the cave and put her arm around Griz's shaking shoulders and saw Bee lying in his large, strong paw.

Bee smiled as she saw the love in Comfort's gaze. "Griz, please take care of my hive. Maybe Comfort can help you."

Griz lay there in a sad stupor over losing his only and remarkable friend, Bee. He vaguely felt the heavy furry arm that rested over him. He felt as if it were Bee's arm as she whispered to him. He was staring at Bee with large tears matting the fur under his eyes. He took a deep breath and realized he was only sorry for himself, his own loss. He was not thinking of Bee. She was trying to comfort him rather than him comforting her. He whispered, "I am sorry Bee, you have been a wonderful friend. You saved my life and you were never thinking of self. You only wanted the best for your hive. You have been my friend and I will always honor you in my memory for that. You may leave now any time that you are ready. Your love, your compassion, your courage and your energy will always be with me. You have fulfilled your purpose. You may go."

"Good bye dear Griz.... I gave you all I had; I gave you my time, my honey, my stinger and my life. Just promise me one thing before I go, please Griz..." squeaked Bee in a tiny faint voice.

"Anything, dear Bee" pleaded Griz.

"Griz, please just look around and see all the gifts you have. Promise me that you will be satisfied and grateful. Enjoy the life you have. The life I have sacrificed my few remaining days to give you. I have nothing more to give." And Bee was no more.

You might think that this is the end of the story and you are right.

Yet memory lingers and the loves of the past create the present.

Years later humans discovered a new "species" of bear living far up in the mountains. This new bear seemed to be a crossbreeding between Grizzlies and Black Bears. More remarkable was the fact that they were totally vegetarian.

To their amazement, humans also discovered honeybees that exclusively created their hives at the mouths of caves where these bears slept for the winter. Also amazingly, the bees seemed to create an extra honeycomb far beyond their needs exclusively for the bears. The bears never touched the honey that the bees needed for themselves. The humans documented by film this very special arrangement within nature and named the documentary "Life is Amazing." Many humans could not understand why this same type of cooperation seemed to be impossible for humans. Some speculated that perhaps humans had not yet evolved to this high order of cooperation and compassion.

A Fishy Story

Once upon a time there was a goldfish named Peter. He lived in a fish bowl with two ferny plants he named Tickle and Sway. Imagining the world outside his bowl was not possible because he had no idea of what lay outside the bedroom door that he saw open and close as a two-legged creature came and went.

One day the two-legged came in and took the bowl to the backyard where there was a small pond. It wished Peter well in his new home and emptied Peter, Tickle and Sway into the pond.

Well, Tickle and Sway loved their new home. They immediately sank their roots into the soft sandy bottom and began soaking up the many rich nutrients from this natural environment that did not exist in the fish tank. They loved the breezes that rippled the water overhead and stirred the water. When the sun beat down they stretched for it and when it rained they felt energized deep within and danced. They were so happy they almost forgot about Peter. Where was he anyway? Oh...Oh...there he is hiding in the shadow of a large rock looking scared and alone. "What's the matter?" they asked.

"Didn't you hear that sound?" he asked.

No, maybe they were too busy stretching and growing to notice.

It sounds like "Crooooooak" Peter added. I think something is waiting to eat me.

They were quiet and listened, but heard nothing. They listened and watched as water spiders glided silently across the surface of the pond. Then a dragonfly softly buzzed down from above and took a long drink.

Tiny little dark fishlike creatures swam by wiggling in a swarm as they passed.

The sky was starting to darken and yellow, pinks and blues reflected from above.

Did Peter need to find a better place to hide?

At that moment there was a fleeting splash at the surface and as quick as a wink a tongue lashed out, caught the dragonfly and stuffed it into a mouth.

"What was that?" exclaimed Tickle. Sway began to cry. Peter cringed closer to the rock feeling very conspicuous in his bright orange body.... "Surely the monster will get me," he thought.

At that moment Bobo, a large koi, slowly swam into view. "This is it!" thought Peter.

"Hey, you there, behind the rock. Yeah, you scaredy pants. No one is going to eat you here unless one of those bass escapes the big pond. That was just Fog, the frog, having his dinner. He only eats the bugs off the top of the water. You're new here, so introduce yourself. I'm Bobo."

Bobo was the wisest, most beloved fish in the pond. His large size set him apart from all the rest, but his wisdom united the pond in one community of love and understanding. Bobo was white except for a black spot on his back that looked like a big eye, and many in the pond believed Bobo could see all with his extra eye. They thought he surely knew everything. As he swam by Peter, Sway and Tickle, they all felt more relaxed and at home in their new pond.

"Hi Bobo, I'm Peter" squeaked Peter timidly. "And this is Tickle and Sway. We are new here. Can you tell me when dinner is served? I am getting really hungry."

Oh...my young lad...I can see you need to learn a bit about this place. First of all there is nothing here that eats any other living thing in the water except Fog and we have no fear of him. This is a harmonious, happy community. This is what they call an ornamental pond. The two-legged mammals have a much larger pond just 400 feet from here where it is survival of the fittest. The bass eat other fish like the bluegill. You are privileged to be here. I suppose it is because of your beautiful color. If you were colorless you would have been put in the dog-eat-dog world of the large pond. Yeah, you are privileged because of your color and don't forget that. We don't even have fish in here that would eat your weed friends. The two-leggeds understand that your weed friends are healthy for our environment and do not want them eaten away. So they also are privileged because there are fish in the large pond that eat nothing but weeds. Now, about food...at the same time every day, the two-leggeds drop food into the water. You have to be careful then because there is a feeding frenzy. No one intends to harm anyone and yet the fish do act crazy. As small and new as you are, you had better stay off the surface and eat only the food that floats down to you. Stay out of the way of the bigger fish. You may unintentionally get hurt. I for one have conquered the frenzy in me. Because I am so big I leisurely go to the top and eat as I please.... So that is the story of eating here. We simply must time our hunger for feeding and be thankful there is plenty without having to die for it. I would say we have about an hour before food arrives. Now relax and enjoy this space you have been given and get to know the others in the pond. Stay

41

colorful and entertain the two-leggeds and you'll be all right here. But if the two-leggeds get tired of you they might net you and take you to the big pond, a dark, scary place where enemies want to eat you at every turn.

Peter was just beginning to relax a little when a two-legged came to the edge of the pond and sprinkled Peter's very favorite food flakes on the surface. Suddenly from out of nowhere fish of all different colors came pushing their way to the food. Peter froze with fear. One or two little flakes drifted down to where he was hiding and he ate them carefully and quietly, hoping no one would notice him. After the fish had dispersed he found a few more crumbs to quiet his growling stomach. Bobo circled back around and Peter pouted and declared angrily, "I hate this pond; I want my fish bowl back. I want food that is just for me, and I want to be the biggest fish around! I want to go home."

"Oh, poor little scaredy-pants" Bobo chided, "Be not afraid. You must give up your old small bowl to become bigger and wiser and more powerful. Staying small is easy, but changing and growing and learning takes courage. Look! You have friends around to help you."

"What friends? What are you talking about? I don't see any friends around here...just a bunch of maniacs when they are hungry...."

"Look," said Bobo, "You hide behind your rock and you haven't reached out to know anyone here. Your best friends are weeds. Have you ever tried to get close to any one of your own species? Yeah, we have an artificial environment here maintained by the two-leggeds. We eat once a day and that is all we get. It is truly unreal. If you want a natural habitat where you don't have feeding frenzy, where you eat all day and at the same time risk being eaten, and then go to the large pond. If all you care about is your belly, that is where you belong. I like your weed friends, but you are a fish and I would think that you would have at least a couple of fish friends."

Just then the Snook Twins, Seiko and Keiko, floated leisurely up to Bobo. They were not really twins but they had close-to-identical coloring. They were goldfish with swirling patches of rich black. Peter was amazed at their beauty.

"Hey Bobo," spoke Seiko Snook, "who is the new fellow? Why hasn't he come around to show himself? He isn't one of those over-privileged rich kids from a fish bowl, is he?"

"Yeah, so what if I come from a fish bowl," retorted Peter as he emerged from his hiding place. "Do I have any choice?"

"Forget that fish bowl where you had everything for yourself." retorted Seiko.

Angered, Peter shouted "Now that I am here, I will show you all what I am made of. I will not just hide behind rocks and wait to die; I will go out and discover this new world of mine! I will go where I have never gone before. Then you will see who the smart one is."

The Snook Twins began to smile, which made Peter more upset, and he began to pop up and down and twirling in circles until suddenly something touched him and he jumped behind his rock.... Then Seiko and Keiko really began to laugh. They were smiling at three wide-eyed tadpoles that were behind Peter and it became so very funny they couldn't help but laugh when one of them touched him while he was trying to act so brave.

Bobo floated gently over to Peter and explained that they were not really laughing at him but at the situation. It was about having a choice about where we come from and then to see those innocent wide-eyed tadpoles behind Peter dancing and imitating him when he was acting so serious. "Please forgive them," requested Bobo.

"All right," answered Peter..."but I am still going to make something out of myself that people will respect."

"Listen," said Bobo." You need do no such thing. We'll accept you exactly the way you are, but you certainly need to develop a sense of humor about yourself. That is really the way we get along in such close quarters, especially during the feeding frenzy. We cannot stop our frenzy even though there is plenty of food...so we simply have to find humor in it...like a game."

Peter's friends, Tickle and Sway, looked on and worried that they were losing their dear friend because now he had other fish to befriend. At least, they had one another.

"OK," said Peter to himself, "First I need to figure out how to be happy in the pond, so I will ask everyone I meet for advice."

"Seiko, are you happy in this pond?" he asked.

"No," she answered, "this pond has no cute boy fish, except you and you are just too little and scared for me."

"I am not happy either," piped in Keiko. "This pond is just too boring for me."

So Peter swam on and found Fog the frog sitting on a log watching for bugs.

"Are you happy in this pond, Fog?"

"Yes," he said. "This pond has sunshine and plenty of food, diversity, peace, cooperation and companionship. I have many happy friends and we do many happy things together. What else could anyone need?"

"OK," Peter said. "Then I need to find happy friends too." And off he swam.

Well...Peter did make friends and grew comfortable within the pond and its community. He also grew in size, not quite as large as Bobo in length and weight and yet stronger and more agile than any fish in the pond. He regularly visited with his friends Tickle and Sway. He played "chase me" with Seiko and Keiko. He received news from the large pond from Fog and the three tadpoles that had now grown into quite handsome frogs. Bobo became his confidant and mentor. He remembered how scared he had been to eat and, having conquered his own frenzy, made sure everyone had enough. When the Great Blue Heron visited the pond he would herd the smaller fish to a deep dark place and then go to the surface to challenge the heron. He so frustrated the heron; it never came to that pond again.

No one noticed at first that Seiko and Keiko were losing their color; gradually they turned dirty-water brown. They were difficult to see by the two-leggeds and yet everyone knew that as soon as they were found out they would be moved to the larger pond. This is what all the fish in the ornamental pond feared: to be left in the wild to survive on their own with predators all around was unthinkable.

"How can we save the Snook twins?" Peter asked Bobo one day.

"Well, they need to appear to be special, I think, for the two-leggeds to leave them in this pond." Bobo replied.

"Special," said Peter over and over to himself. He swam around for days with only "special" on his mind. Suddenly it came to him; he would make dresses for them out of fern leaves to make them look very fancy. He took this idea to Tickle and Sway, and they were less than enthusiastic, fearing that it might hurt to give up some of their branches.

"Our fronds!" exclaimed Tickle and Sway in unison.

"Dressed in fern," retorted Seiko and Keiko, "that is disgusting!"

"Our fronds are not disgusting. They are beautiful. You will turn them into lifeless clothing on your ugly body." shouted Tickle.... "Besides...do you think it will be comfortable cutting our long beautiful fronds? It'd take forever to grow them back."

"No way, we won't do it," yelled Seiko, and both Seiko and Keiko gave Peter, Tickle and Sway their tail and quickly swam away in a huff.

Peter felt as alone as he had ever been.

Seiko and Keiko looked at each other and smiled. "Maybe we should tell Peter that we are loosing our color because we are getting ready to lay eggs," suggested Seiko.

"No, it is just too fun to tease him," said Keiko. "Let's see what wild scheme he will come up with next."

"You are so mean, Keiko. Can't you see how worried he is? He is afraid of losing us. He will be so excited to know that there will be more goldfish in the pond this spring. Tickle and Sway will be so proud to have the chance to hide our eggs in their fronds; we are all lucky that Peter did not start ripping them apart! Let's tell him."

"Wait a second," murmured Bobo as he slowly ascended from beneath them. First of all you two are too close to the surface for your safety. Second, that is an old wives' tale about changing colors because you're laying eggs. Now I don't think you're sick nor do I believe you have parasites. So there is only one answer: genetics. You will naturally turn darker, and that is nothing to be ashamed of. Yet there is always the threat of the two-leggeds, so be careful." And with that Bobo sauntered away.

Suddenly there was a loud thrash of water and a net swooped down from above. Yet before Seiko and Keiko could react a flash of gold torpedoed straight for the net and pushed it away. At first they were stunned and unable to move, but given that bit of time they dove for a deep shadowy place. Was that Peter who saved them from the net? Did the net get him? They peeked up and saw Peter in the net. The two-leggeds turned the net over and dumped Peter back into the water and walked away.

Peter was quite pleased with himself and started to tease Seiko for being so stupid as to show herself. Then he started to bump and chase her. "Seiko, you are so silly," Peter said as he bumped her again.

"Oh Peter," Seiko blushed, "Why are you bumping me like that?"

As Peter bumped her again out came some little jellylike balls.

"Oh my," said Peter. "Are you losing your scales?"

Just as he asked, a milky liquid oozed in a path behind him covering the little balls.

Seiko and Keiko together chimed "Oh my" with wide-open eyes. "I think you are losing something too" said Keiko.

Just then, Bobo came lumbering into view, "You silly innocent young ones. No, don't tell me you didn't feel something between the two of you, Seiko, when Peter bumped you. And Peter, I am sure you had an unusual feeling when you were excited to bump her. That feeling is more than friendship. Although you have a very nice friendship, this is more serious business. Seiko, you just released eggs into the water and, Peter, you covered her eggs with milt. Those eggs will grow into tiny new fish and they will be half Seiko and half Peter, a combination of the two of you."

Peter was aghast and Seiko quickly hid behind Tickle and Sway.

Keiko looked a bit upset and sputtered out, "Nobody told us...how were we to know?"

"Whether you know or not, it seems to come naturally," responded Bobo lightheartedly. "This is a great event.... Now our next problem is that it is natural for you to eat some of those eggs."

"Oooh no!" screamed Seiko," No one will eat my offspring."

"Well that is a new thought," said Bobo. "That will be difficult to stop...even yourself...because it's natural."

"I don't care if it's natural," Peter butted in. "Those small fry are half me and I am strong enough to protect them from anyone, even myself."

"Well I don't know," said Bobo, "No one has ever talked like this before...we simply let nature take its course. There is a down side to your plan and that is, if all the small fry live, we will have too many fish in the pond and we do not know what the two-leggeds would do about that. Would they give us more food? And even if they did there still needs to be a limit as to how many this little pond can hold."

"I don't care," said Peter, and he swam up next to Seiko.

"I will protect your little eggs," Peter declared as he swam back and forth rigidly patrolling his new responsibilities.

"Me too," echoed Seiko as she followed him proudly.

So they continued to patrol together the first day, but the second day they decided they needed to take turns. As time went by they both grew tired and began to close their eyes occasionally while on duty. They would wake up with a start, as they noticed some of Bobo's cousins coming to snack on their eggs. Eventually many of them had been eaten, but a few well hidden in Tickle and Sway's fronds survived.

Finally the day came and ten little goldfish began to swim around them.

"There are still many dangers," warned Bobo. "You must not name them until they survive their first month. It would be bad luck. "

Peter and Seiko were proud of their brood. Yet, for some unknown reason three more died...one simply disappeared and everyone blamed Fog for that. Only Peter refused to believe that Fog would do such a thing. The seven remaining grew into happy little carefree fish under the protection of their strong papa and playful mother.

Suddenly one day a crisis came to the pond. The two-leggeds had not come to the pond in three days; the fish had to begin to forage and eat stuff they had never eaten before. They found some floating plants to be tasty and nutritious, as well as worms and bugs and other stuff that blew into the pond. Fog said he had seen the two-leggeds take all their belongings and leave. Their home was empty.

Many of the fish were beginning to change their color and become lethargic. Bobo took ill. He was very old. Peter sculled in the water next to him. Bobo told Peter that the time had come for him to float to the surface and await death.

Then Bobo confided in Peter the biggest secret ever. He said few would understand that there was no death or birth. We are all part of the same energy...fish, frogs, snakes, birds, the animals that came to drink at the pond, and the two-leggeds. Spiritually we are all one and part of the same energy source that the two-leggeds call God. It is our destiny to understand that no matter how that source manifests itself we are bound to love, compassion and forgiveness because we are all one. No matter what happens to the pond or in the pond we are not to be fearful or angry. Simply realize all existence has one source. With that Bobo told Peter to stay put as he floated up to give his spirit to the universe and his body to the earth.

"No fear, no anger?" Peter questioned as he viewed Bobo floating on the top of the water above him. "How can that be?" he wondered. He was already feeling afraid and angry that Bobo had left him and he had not enough time to get answers to all his questions, much less to figure out what all the questions were.

"What's wrong, Daddy?" asked Meiko.

"Bobo has left us, son, and I have so many questions to ask him." Peter replied.

"Oh, we all have answers Daddy."

"Why do you think so, Meiko?"

"Fog told me as he was eating Leiko the other day."

"What?"

"Yeah, I asked him why he was eating Leiko and he said that I already know the answers to all my questions I said, 'Yeah, we goldfish are too many and you are hungry. Little fish are food for you.'" "You got it," he told me. Well, I know that I am going to be very careful so I can grow to be a big fish and not breakfast."

Just then Eieko and Bieko swiftly swam up to Peter. "Daddy, daddy, daddy.... there are two-leggeds throwing tons of food into the pond.... Look daddy, look."

Peter looked up and saw hundreds of little wafers of food floating and then gently sinking into the water. Food surrounded them all, in every direction food. No one need even move to eat....

Peter hustled about, telling everyone that they should not eat too much or they would become sick.

From then on every day, twice a day, food was thrown into the pond. Peter kept warning everyone not to become dependent on this two-leggeds' food, that they should continue to eat small green floating plants, worms and bugs and be prepared to forage on their own if the two-leggeds ever stopped feeding them.

Peter also noticed the necessity that some eggs be eaten. The pond would simply be too crowded and polluted if every egg were to hatch a newborn. He also came to understand that the heron, the ducks and the frogs needed to eat, and they will eat some fish.

Peter kept hearing Bobo's words repeating in his head, "No anger and no fear...no birth and no death." He began to hold discussion sessions with small groups of the pond fish to share the wisdom he had learned from Bobo as well as his own life.

Peter and Seiko had many offspring and yet only a few would live to maturity. "It was nature's way," said Peter.

The new two-leggeds never brought a net to the pond and respected all the fish whatever there color or size. They were fed very well.

Peter and Seiko lived into old age until it was their turn to float to the surface and release their spirit to the universe and their bodies to the earth....

And what about Meiko, Beiko, and Eeiko?

Well, that is a whole other story....

Hiking with Griz

Griz was a very handsome dark brown grizzly bear. He was tall and strong and robust. He loved to hike and eat. He could not help but smile as he strolled along. He would break into song on particularly pleasant-feeling days like today. Today, he was singing "On the Sunny Side of the Street" when he came across a small striped garter snake sunning itself across the road.

As the bear approached, the snake lazily opened just one eye to see if he would be stepped on, too tired to hardly even care. The winter had been cold and the spring sun felt so wonderful, soaking through his skin and warming him all the way through. On second thought, "Maybe I should wiggle a little just to let the bear know I am here and not to be stepped on." So snake flinched a little from his middle to alert the bear.

Griz noticed the snake and laughed. "Ho, ho, little snake," he laughed. "It is a perfect day for sunning one's self." His song changed to "You Are My Sunshine."

The little snake's eyes kept blinking, fluttering. He could not stop them. This jolly singing bear was too much. He had never seen such a sight or heard such a voice, a deep guttural soft whisper.

Griz always sang softly because he did not want to alert the other bears to the fact that he enjoyed singing. He tried not to be too jolly with them either.

Griz sat himself down on the path and then sprawled himself out flat so that he could be eye to eye with the little snake. He stopped singing and asked, "Little snake, what is your name and what are you doing here? I almost squashed you."

"Aaahhhh," yawned the snake with a large open mouth. Griz thought he could see almost into his stomach from where he lay.

"My friends call me Snoozy," he said "and I am here because it is warm, sunny and dry. The woods are dark and wet and I was chilled all the way through last night, and most of the winter. Now is the time to absorb as much of this beautiful sunshine as I can find. When I am warm enough I will go have a nice lunch of my favorite bugs."

"Bugs, yuck.... Huckleberries are the best food around here, have you tried them?" suggested Griz.

"Yes, but they do not agree with me. Different strokes for different folks, my friend," said Snoozy with a smile as he wiggled a little to get more comfortable.

"Well, my little friend Snoozy, here's the deal.... If you lie here for very long, sooner or later another bear, or moose, elk or deer, or some two-legged will come by and squash you. I have a suggestion. Not far from here, there is an outcropping of rocks warmed from morning till night by the sun and full of various bugs and rodents within its crevices. I also like to snooze there because all around these rocks are large shady trees and berry bushes. There is a pool of cool water from which to drink. If you climb up onto my furry back I'll take you there.... What do you think?"

Snoozy lay there and thought long and hard....

Maybe Griz wants to take me home and feed me to his cubs....

Maybe Mrs. Griz has been wanting a new snake skin purse....

It was a huge risk trusting a grizzly bear, but the rewards could be huge also. Then he realized Griz could just as well have stepped on him and done as he wished with his remains. Maybe he could trust this grizzly bear.

"OK, Griz, but please be gentle with me," said Snoozy as he shimmied up Griz's leg and onto his back.

They hiked and hiked and finally approached a clearing where Snoozy spied two little cubs. They ran to Griz and cried "Daddy, Daddy we are hungry, do you have anything to eat?"

Oh no, thought Snoozy.

"What is that on your back, Dad?" cried Fuzz Bear. "Is it friend or food?" asked Plump Bear.

"Look you guys, this is my friend Snoozy. She is a snake and I invited her to live on the rocks. If you're hungry start down the trail to the huckleberries and I'll be with you right away. Snoozy, you enjoy yourself here; but keep an eye out for the hawk that circles above. Stay close to a crevice so that you can quickly wiggle into it if you catch sight of the hawk.

I'm going down there with my little guys. See ya later...."

Snoozy stretched out on a big rock and yawned. As he watched the bears below he thought to himself, "I guess others really don't know who I am at all. Griz thinks I am a girl; of course these things are hard to tell when you are a snake and have a name like Snoozy. And my friends think I am sleepy all the time. The truth is that I meditate, I am relaxed and I like to absorb my surroundings. Perhaps I am more awake than they are."

He enjoyed lying there on the rock but no one walked by. Snoozy decided he liked the traffic on the road he had been on, so he slithered back to where Griz had found him.

Griz and his cubs returned to the rocks sleepy and ready for an afternoon nap with berry-filled bellies. However, they soon regained all their energy as they frantically searched for Snoozy. He (or she as they thought) was nowhere to be found. Finally Griz concluded that the hawk had claimed Snoozy for lunch. He felt sad for his new friend. They had hardly begun to know one another. He knew he could learn much from this snake-kind so different from himself. He hugged his little bears and reminded them that this is the nature of life: living and dying, friends coming and going, so much of life changing all the time.

Meanwhile Snoozy was attempting to find a comfortable spot on the road to sleep when the earth trembled and great roaring sounds came down the path. He scrambled off the path and it seemed no matter which way he turned, two-leggeds with great machines were tearing down the forest creating large paths and great open areas, destroying all that was his home. He only had thoughts of escaping to the outcropping of rocks high above these weapons of mass destruction, the rocks where bear and his cubs lived. He saw panicked forest creatures scattering in all directions; some into the path of the great machines and crushed instantly. He stayed right on course for the rocks.

Snoozy had never moved so fast. Adrenaline pulsed through him, pushing him faster and faster as he raced back to the grizzly bear home. As he reached them he had no more breath to speak but his eyes told Griz of the danger coming. They all listened to Snoozy's gasping breaths and the crunch and rumble of the destructive machinery. All eyes were large with fear, all hearts pounded in chests, all minds searched for the perfect plan.

"The cave," yelled Griz. "Head for the cave," he instructed as he tossed Snoozy on his back and grabbed Fuzz and Plump.

"Will Mommy be OK?" asked Plump.

"Oh yes, Plump," replied Griz. "She is already in the cave getting a surprise ready for us!"

They were within plain sight of the cave when Griz abruptly halted.... He told Plump and Fuzz to join their mommy for the surprise and to tell her he would be along soon. He must go back and see what the two-leggeds were up to. The kids ran ahead as they were told; Griz and Snoozy headed back to their rock overlook.

Once there, they watched the two-leggeds gradually move up the mountain with their machinery. Griz could see that they would be stopped as they came up against the high wall of rock, which protected his domain. Regardless, he paced back and forth, growling and bellowing in a great state of agitation, almost stepping on Snoozy several times. He knew he could easily kill many of the two-leggeds. They were nothing without their machines.

Snoozy worked his way up to a very high rock and called down to Griz, "Hey Griz, there is a different kind of two-legged down there and coming this way." Griz stopped and focused on the place that Snoozy pointed out. Sure enough there was a two-legged with nothing on but shorts covering the middle part of his body. All the other two-leggeds had red hard hats, a yellow covering over their whole body and black heavy footgear. This odd two-legged had a long stick in his hand as he crisscrossed the hillside. He was forcing all the animals—deer, rabbit, coon, coyote and more, even a couple of small black bear up to the safety of the rocks and the forests beyond. He was quick, agile and fast.... If a rabbit headed back down in panic into the danger he could catch up to it and turn it around. Then to his continued surprise Griz saw two dogs helping him herd all the forest animals to safety.

They watched the two-legged for a long time and saw hundreds of animals pass through a gap in the stone wall and up the forest animal path to the high ground. Knowing that they were safe from the destruction below, they stalked the two-legged to see what he would do next. To Griz's surprise the two-legged lay down by the same pool of water that Griz drank from. The two-legged was very thirsty and drank for a long time before rolling over on his back and resting on the moss bank. Then two others dressed the same as him came out of the forest with gear for sheltering and food. One was female of the species. The two dogs were with them. Griz and Snoozy stayed under cover and were in awe of these two-leggeds who seem to love the forest and its animals. They watched them sit by their campfire eating dried fruits, vegetable and nuts. Griz and Snoozy had never been this close to observe two-leggeds before and were indeed surprised at how comfortable they were with them. Of course this must be a much different species from others they had known.

Fuzz had arrived at the mouth of the dark cave first, out of breath from running as fast as his little legs could carry him. Even though he had wanted to beat Plump to the surprise, he would not enter without his brother. As he waited he could hear voices from inside. The familiar voice of his mother sounded especially cheerful. He heard a new voice; it was very low and booming with a particularly dramatic flair.

Plump finally jogged up and whined, "Why didn't you wait for me, Fuzz?"

"SSHHH" whispered Fuzz, "Someone is there with Momma! Listen."

They heard a deep thunderous laugh from inside the cave that welcomed them to come inside. But before they could muster the courage, out stepped an ancient grizzly that embraced them and boomed..."Well, there are my big handsome grandsons! How did you get so big? There must be mountains of berry patches here to produce bears like this!"

Right behind him emerged Momma with a proud smile.

Fuzz suddenly remembered his Dad.

"Momma, Daddy and his friend Snoozy are going to investigate some big machines and horrible noises coming from the forest."

The wolf, Caboul, padded softly up behind Griz and Snoozy.... He and Griz had made peace and were friends.

"What is this snake doing here? I eat snakes."

"Shh," softly whispered Griz. "We are watching those two-leggeds down there, and leave the snake alone. He is my friend, Snoozy."

"Since when do you keep the company of snakes?" snickered Caboul. "Ahh it doesn't matter...there is plenty else to eat, like small bear...."

"Cut the joking around," retorted Griz. "There are serious happenings in the forest. The two-leggeds are destroying our habitat. Then we found this different species of two-leggeds who seem to be kind to animals."

"I know all about it," said Caboul. "Very few know that I was orphaned by two-leggeds who killed my mother, father and most of my pack. I was very young and almost died of starvation when some two-legged found me, took me home, raised me and then sent me back into the forest. I know better than any of you about the two types of two-leggeds. All I can suggest is stay away from the evil ones and be nice to the good ones. The problem is sometimes you cannot tell them apart. See ya later.... I'm off to see what is happening in other parts of the forest."

As Caboul trotted off, Griz turned to Snoozy and suggested they go to his cave to rest.

Snoozy was too curious about the two-leggeds they were watching to leave. He told Griz to go along without him. That is what Griz did.

Snoozy found a comfortable place to curl up to watch the activities below, but to his surprise the two-leggeds crawled into their tent, made a few soft hums and sighs and became quiet. What, no big fire, no bottle smashing, no loud shouts and screams? Somehow Snoozy was pleased and started his way up the hill to Griz's cave.

As he approached he could hear a wise old voice telling stories of love and courage, and the cubs cheering approvingly. A glow came from the opening, encouraging Snoozy to go inside and curl up by Griz.

Griz was embarrassed when Snoozy simply slithered into the cave and nonchalantly cuddled up to him. Momma Bear screamed thinking that Snoozy might bite him. She relaxed when Griz gave her big smile and assured her that Snoozy was his friend. Grandpa Bear immediately began a story about a snake that had been his friend when he was a young bear. The tiny snake had warned him of a bear trap on the trail; that warning probably saved him. They hung around together for a year and then went their separate ways. The young bears fell asleep, and grandpa was getting tired. He said that he would wander off the next morning to see what was happening in other parts of the forest. All was well in that snug little cave that night as everyone fell into a deep slumber....

The Shopkeeper's Son

He was a moderately wealthy merchant. His shop contained a variety of useful household items. However, because of his shop, he could not travel to visit relatives who lived a long way off in another district.

This merchant had one child, a son, about sixteen years of age. The father decided that his son was old enough to care for the shop so that he and his wife could visit relatives.

All arrangements having been made, the merchant and his wife set out to visit family, and the son remained behind to tend the shop. The father had not realized that he had spoiled the boy. He had given his son anything he wanted from the time he was born. He wished the boy to be always happy. The boy, accustomed to being given everything he desired, had become lazy and lacked responsibility.

In the first days after his parents leaving, the boy tended the shop at the prescribed hours. However, having developed bad habits, he eventually remained away from the shop for longer and longer periods of time. Whatever profits he made from the shop he used to stay out very late drinking with his friends. He would come into the shop late every day or not at all.

Friends of the father noticed what was happening and sent him letters warning that his business was in ruin. The father did not believe the letters. When he returned home he found his son drunk in bed, the shop closed and no money from sales.

The father was furious with his son and threw him out of the house saying: "Until you learn to be responsible and do your duty, you are not my son." Of course, soon after the son was gone the father regretted his rage. He wanted only happiness for his son.

The son wandered for three years. He met people who shared drugs and alcohol. He stole money and food to support his habits. One cold, rainy windy day he huddled under several layers of cardboard to keep dry and warm, having not eaten in three days and having no money for drugs and alcohol.

An old man hobbled up to him and presented him with a note. "You are to meet death tonight at 7:00 PM on the mountain. Do not be late."

The boy now a young man thought, "So it has come to this. My life has been suffering. I will be relieved of my suffering. This is my appointment. I will not be late."

The young man was one-half hour early for his appointment with death. He was eager to get it over with. He had washed his body and clothes. He was ready to end his life of suffering.

Suddenly, the same old man who had given him the note appeared.

The young man embraced the old man: "So you are death. You may take me now. I am ready to end my sufferings." The old man drew back and laughed, "Indeed I am death but I take no one."

The young man became excited, "Go ahead! Kill me."

Again the old man laughed, even louder: "I am death but I do not kill anyone."

"Then why I am here?" shouted the young man, "I want to die. I want to end my sufferings."

The old man responded gently. "It is not my job to take your life. You sow the seed of your own destruction. You will kill yourself; I come only to ease your transition into the next life."

The young man begged the old man, "Please, please death, take me now."

The old man put his arm around the young man: "If you were to die now you would be reincarnated into worse misery. You have done nothing with your precious gift of this life. You will suffer much more in the next. You are young and not ready to die. The seeds of your destruction have grown long but are not yet full-grown. There is time for you, time enough to cut down what you have grown and time enough to cultivate new seeds that will enable you to live a full good life now and in the hereafter. Go home. Change your life."

With that, the old man disappeared. The young man returned home and was welcomed by his father with open arms, and yet his father distrusted his son. To regain his trust the father asked his son to perform a dangerous task. The father had been told that an evil man wished to kill him. He was to meet the evil man at 12:00 noon on the next day. The father asked his son to go in his place and find out from the man why he wished to kill the father.

Confident because he had already met death and survived, the son arrived to meet the evil man ten minutes early. He waited for three hours and the evil man never came. Every day for two weeks the young man waited at twelve noon for three hours and the evil man did not come. The father was elated with his son's steadfastness. The father was also satisfied that the story of the evil man was just rumor with no foundation. The young man had earned his father's respect and was put in care of the shop once again. His father and mother would travel to visit relatives. The father also promised his son he would find a wife for him.

The boy learned from death that he sows his own seeds of destruction. He was determined to cultivate only good seeds and live a long, full life.

One day a well-dressed man and his beautiful daughter entered the shop. He asked to see the shop owner. The young man told him that his father was away but that he had authority to sell whatever the man wanted. Because of the young man's days of wandering he had become experienced in recognizing people who were trouble. He judged the rich man to be trouble.

The well-dressed man brought his beautiful daughter forward. He told the young man that he would very much like for his daughter and the young man to know one another better. He told the young man that he was wealthy and he should like the young man to come with him now to live with them.

The young man had his mind set on doing what was right and was determined not to betray his father's trust. Attending the shop was more important than going with the man and his daughter. His father would return soon and he will have found him a wife.

The young man decided to be direct and asked, "Are you he who my father was to meet and never came?" The rich man answered, "Yes I am he, but I was called out of town for a while and have now returned to bargain with your father; his life for your happiness."

Young man: "I am not unhappy!"

Rich Man: "Would you not be happier with my daughter and my riches?"

Young man: "Acchha...I see who you are. You are the seed of my father's own destruction. He loves me so much he would give his life for my happiness."

The young man began to laugh. He laughed louder and louder.

The angry rich man asked, "Why do you laugh? Look at my daughter. Look at my wealth; do you not wish to posses them?"

Young man: "I have met death and he explained to me the seeds of destruction. I no longer seek my own happiness. I am happy when I can help others. I am at peace. My father does not need to bargain with you and neither do I. Get out of here!" With that, the rich man disappeared.

Trail Dancer

A soft warm rain along the rocky trail that heads up the mountain above the Kangra Valley settled the dust and brought the fresh scent of moist soil, newly energized vegetation and fragrant flowers. The rain thrilled my skin as it soaked through my clothes and brought relief from the dry dusty heat of the past months, my face dripping with the tickling droplets of refreshing sky water. It was then that I saw her dancing down the path. Her sari swayed as her body danced; legs, arms, head, and hips ecstatic with joy. My heart leapt as she danced by me with a caressing smile. I watched her dance down the path to the valley. She was a cherished memory of my time in India.

The next time I saw her, I was hiking a rugged mountain trail in North Idaho. I was alone, separated from the other hikers since I had stopped to take pictures of bear grass. This time she was dressed with hiking sandals, heavy brown shorts and flannel shirt, her hair pulled back instead of the loose cascade that was in India.... I knew it was the same woman. Her dance was different but the body the same, her head thrown back and then forward into that same embracing smile for me and for all life the same ecstatic joy.

The third and last time I saw her was when visiting my daughter in Tucson, Arizona. She was a friend of my daughter's whom I met at the trailhead of Sabino Canyon. I knew she looked familiar and yet I could not place her. She was dressed with running shoes, tight running pants and a runner's tank top. She and my daughter ran ahead as I walked the trail. As I watched them from a distance, I saw her begin to dance and I knew it was the same woman I had met twice before. Even from that distance I could see her look back and smile at all that is.... When we met at the end of the trail I was too timid to ask her about our previous meetings. I did see her one more time at an outdoor dance festival as she gave her body generously and with abandon to the dance.

Ahhhhhhh! Was it really the same woman in each of those instances? Or was it the enlightened spirit of love and joy, which bewitched three different women. Is not life a trail dance from here to there?

Owl and Squirrel

In the past, when hunting bats, Owl always stopped at the cave's entrance. This evening, however, he had no idea why he followed Bat into the cave. Once inside, Bat disappeared and the darkness was much blacker than a moonless, starless night. Owl did not understand why he continued forward deeper into the cave to find an escape rather than retrace his flight back to the entrance. His wings swiped sharp rocks and dead ends loomed ahead at every turn. He squeezed through crevices and bounced off protruding rock formations. Fear entered his heart, and his natural instincts as well as his night vision failed him. His strong will alone drove him further into the blackness.

Finally, dim light revealed an opening into a small rocky canyon. Yet, the canyon was almost as dark as the cave. There did not seem to be a sky overhead, only blackness that forced his vision downwards towards the canyon floor. Suddenly, a small animal ran beneath him. Normally, the owl would have seen that little mammal before it even thought of running. Normally, Owl would have silently glided into the animal's path, clenched it in his talons and carried it away for a feast. This night however was different. Fear had taken hunger as well as his instincts for the hunt from him. He had seen no other living creature since he had entered the cave and was surprised at his reaction to the little animal. The small creature no longer existed to satisfy his appetite. He needed a companion in this desolate world.

For a moment, from the corner of his eye, Owl saw the little animal, a squirrel, sitting on a rock ledge chattering at him. It quickly disappeared. The owl flew further down the canyon and for a split second entered broad daylight. Although a nocturnal animal, he welcomed its presence. No sooner had he rejoiced in the light than he was immersed in a dark forest. Its canopy created a black dome over him. Again, Owl could see only the ground below. The squirrel sat beneath a large tree chattering at him and then quickly ran up the tree and out of sight.

The lonely, grieving owl needed to see that squirrel again. He flew to a branch, rested there and opened his wings wide and invited the squirrel to come to him. In every possible way he tried to assure the squirrel that he would not eat him or harm him in any way. From out of nowhere, the squirrel seemed to float through the air and cuddle in the warmth of the big bird's wings. The owl discovered a simple, uncomplicated, inclusive wisdom. He carried this wisdom within his heart and mind the rest of his life. He warned fledgling owls of the cave, but he never forbade them to enter.

Hoop Tree

The dilapidated pickup truck crawled up the hill and swung off the pavement into two deep ruts that lead to the Yazzie home, a traditional eight-sided log and mud hogan. The truck twisted and bumped its way through the darkness, headlights wildly stabbing at the fleeting silhouettes of rocks, scrub-brush and pinion pine. Kee Richard felt cold steel on his backside as a jolt of the truck tore the blanket beneath him from its comfortable place. Kee Richard pulled a portion of blanket from beneath his grandma to cover the cold spot and leaned closer to her. The long ride from the YeiiBicheii ceremony on Pine Ridge to his home on Low Mountain had been no more or less uncomfortable than others. His father had drunk too much cheap wine and yet was capable of keeping the vehicle on the road and finding his way home. Kee Richard's older brother, Wayne, sat up front with his father. His grandma, his little sister and his mother huddled with him in the open bed of the truck. This was the usual way.

Kee Richard had slept for most of the three-hour ride with the cold mountain air whistling around him as the truck hurried down the smooth highway. For the next half-hour as the truck struggled through the maze of tracks that led into the roadless countryside and eventually to his home, Kee Richard thought about the weekend and the healing ceremony for his cousin Norman. Norman and he had spent the last two summers herding sheep in the mountain pasture. Now Norman lay inside his family's hogan unconscious of this world. For eight days the medicine man, singers and dancers drew sand paintings, sang and danced to bring Norman from his dream world.

Norman was four years older than Kee Richard. He had been breaking a horse to saddle when he was thrown and hit his head on a rock. The crystal gazer indicated that the accident might have happened because Norman had watched a she-bear give birth. If Norman did not recover soon and his life seemed to be slipping away, he would be taken to the Public Health Hospital.

These thoughts brought to Kee Richard's mind the confusion he had over the Navajo way and the Anglo way. The white doctors would treat Norman quite differently than the medicine man. Even among the older people there were many arguments as to how to treat the sick or injured. Many Navajo used both, and Kee Richard wondered if Norman should also have that benefit.

This conflict between Navajo and Anglo way reminded Kee Richard of the fact that he would be leaving for a Bureau of Indian Affairs boarding school soon. Because of the vast network of good roads that the tribe had built, there were not many boarding schools remaining. However, Kee Richard's home on Low Mountain was two hours from the nearest day school. There was no choice but to live at the school in order to comply with the law.

The idea of living at the boarding school was extremely disturbing to Kee Richard. The large sterile dormitory room filled with students was not as comfortable as his family's one-room hogan. Sitting at a desk in school was extremely difficult for a boy comfortable with roaming the mountains. Glared at and ridiculed by teachers and others because he could not read, write or speak English well enough filled him with a silent anger and withdrawal from everyone. Those Anglos pointed at him, looked him in the eye and asked difficult questions of him without regard for the Navajo way of respecting one another. Kee Richard knew that this year at boarding school would be the same as the last—a painful nightmare until he returned to his family.

Kee Richard consciously fought to keep his mind off the future, the boarding school. He forced his thought back to the YeiiBicheii ceremony, the long hours of sitting while his older brother and father sang and danced with the men. He spent many hours wandering nearby canyons avoiding the ruins left by the Anasazi—the ancient ones. At night at the periphery of the fire he stole gulps of wine from unattended bottles to warm his body and encourage sleep.

Suddenly the truck stopped, the engine turned off and then silence—the blessed silence of Low Mountain. He felt the shake of the truck and heard the slam of the door as his father and brother left the cab. His grandmother, mother and sister began to stir. He must haul some firewood and begin a fire so that his mother could roast a little mutton. That is what he did.

Now in late summer, the boarding school was as frightening as ever for Kee Richard with one exception. Tall, lanky, blonde-headed Mark Miller, the physical education instructor, did not point or look at him and only on occasion spoke to him. He did not force Kee Richard to participate. He did not single Kee Richard out because of his height; he simply made encouraging remarks in passing when no one would notice.

Mark had made some innovations in the physical education program. He built an obstacle course similar to what marines might use in basic training. Mark also welded together a series of basketball hoops that varied in height. This made it easier for the smaller kids to shoot and even dunk. Mark allowed the older boys to build a bucking horse with a fifty-gallon drum, rope and car springs mounted between two large trees. In physical education class, just as in his other classes, Kee Richard did very little. Yet, on his own when no one was looking he would run the obstacle course and dunk dirt clods.

Mark Miller was responsible for a section of the dormitory where thirty boys slept. His window was opposite the field and the cottonwoods where he had created the obstacle course. It was an interesting and difficult course which ran through the woods, over dead trees, down the creek bed, over the creek, across a field with walls to climb and trenches to clear, back over the creek by rope and a straight away dash to the finish. Mark rose early each morning to indulge himself in quiet time before reveille for the dormitory. Consequently, he was the only person in the world to see Kee Richard gracefully and quickly run the obstacle course. He watched for several mornings until it occurred to him to pull out his stopwatch and time the boy. He was fast; however Mark was even more impressed with the style of the boy's run—relaxed, graceful and with extremely efficient use of energy. He began to wonder how he could involve this boy in sports and in particular the cross-country team he was forming for the first time at the school. Mark was new to the school; he was not new to the reservation. He had taught a year previously at another BIA school where he was not allowed to try anything new. He knew it was not difficult to get the boys to participate in sports because they had little else to do at the boarding school. However, it was almost impossible to motivate traditional Navajo kids like Kee Richard to reach their potential, to drive themselves towards personal goals, to stand out among others, to be recognized for their talent. It wasn't the Navajo way.

These thoughts reminded Mark that not many students had signed up for cross-country, only three to be exact.

There may be other students besides Kee Richard who had talent and yet would not compete. Mark decided that he would take his physical education classes on long runs, discover who had ability and find some way for them to join his team.

On the third day of the P.E. run, Mark was beginning to see who had talent, and yet hadn't decided how he could approach them to run for his team. The run began as usual—a long leisurely run down the flat road and a short climb up the first hill. Here, all stopped to stretch and prepare their bodies for a more vigorous run across the hill country strewn with rocks and boulders, cut up by deep gouges in the earth from mountain snow run-off and populated by greasewood, sage brush, cactus, and cedar. As usual Mark, a young man in his early twenties, could keep the pace. However, as usual there were also a few students who could not simply run with the pack. They ran off on forty-five or ninety degree angles chasing jack rabbits and were lost from sight until they appeared again a hundred yards ahead of the pack. On this day, Kee Richard joined this elite group. Mark realized that the only way he could get Kee Richard and the others like him on his team would be through the three boys who had already signed up. They had to be treated as a group, not as individuals. This thinking was opposite to that which Mark experienced as a young man.

Mark ended up with ten boys on his cross-country team and had a very successful year. He sent two boys to the state championships. Kee Richard was not one of them. Kee Richard had always placed well in the meets; however he did not have the will to win, to be a standout. Kee Richard simply liked running with the group.

During the cross-country season, Mark found he could talk to Kee Richard as long as he didn't pressure him, look him in the eye or point at him. They didn't talk about themselves, or one another. They only talked of what they could see together. Because of Kee Richard's height Mark began to eye him for his basketball team. When time came for the physical education class to play basketball Kee Richard did not participate. Mark felt that he couldn't directly approach him concerning the team. Furthermore Kee Richard's grades were very poor and some of the teachers had objected to him running cross-country. The school year became just another year of frustration for Mark. His basketball team was four and twelve on the season with the tallest and perhaps one of the most athletic boys unapproachable.

When school closed for the summer, Kee Richard came home with a plan. He had enjoyed shooting baskets at the school when no one was looking. He decided he would find a way to set up a hoop near his family's hogan. In early June, the Yazzie family piled into their pickup truck for a weekend in Gallup, New Mexico. His father aimed to sell jewelry he had made during the winter and his mother would sell Navajo fry bread that she freshly made using a Coleman stove and an iron skillet and sold off the tailgate of the truck. These trips were important supplements to the family income. When they arrived in Gallup, Kee Richard was free to roam. He spent most of his time at the landfill where he hoped to find a basketball hoop amidst the trash. He found one, backboard and all. Even though the backboard was simply four weather-beaten boards nailed together and the hoop had two broken brackets, it was exactly what he was looking for. He knew his Uncle Charlie Pete had welding equipment and could easily fix the brackets. Kee Richard did not think a net was necessary. Now all he needed was a long four-by-four to sink into the ground. He was sure he could obtain one for free at the lumber mill. He had been there a few times with his uncle and had seen a large pile of discarded wood. A basketball? He would use dirt clods and stones until he could find a way of obtaining a basketball. Kee Richard's father said nothing as he loaded the backboard and hoop into the pickup. That was his way.

Luckily Charlie Pete, Kee Richard's uncle, was heading for the sawmill on the very next weekend and told the boy that he would find a four-by-four for him. Charlie Pete was a more modern Navajo than Kee Richard's father. Charlie had finished school and learned a trade. Kee Richard found himself fortunate to have an uncle who was a little more knowledgeable about the white man's ways. In fact it was Charlie Pete who had convinced the parents of Norman Yazzie to take him to an Anglo doctor after the healing ceremony. As it happened, Norman completely recovered. When the men drank too much, they would argue whether the ceremony or the Anglo medicine had cured Norman. Kee Richard began to think that there was something to learn from both ways; however, his feelings were purely Navajo.

The Yazzie hogan was approximately six miles from the paved road on a high and barren plateau that dropped off into an arroyo with cottonwoods behind the sheep corral. Mountains and red cliffs were a far sight across an arid valley. From this place one could view Father-sky from horizon to horizon, observing storm clouds forming eighty miles away, and as many as four rainbows simultaneously after a cloud burst. As the sun moved across the sky, the appearance of the desert was in constant change. In this place, on a flat sandy area Kee Richard planted his "hoop tree," as strange and out of place as the towers that held the electric power lines that cross Navajo land.

Uncle Charlie Pete helped Kee Richard. He liked the idea of the boy shooting baskets. Charlie bought a bag of cement to hold the post and, to Kee Richard's great surprise, a basketball. Charlie was Kee Richard's mother's youngest brother. He was the first of their family to finish high school. He had played basketball on Ganado High School's basketball team. Like Kee Richard, he was taller than the average Navajo; however he never had the opportunity or the talent to become a good player. He liked the idea that he could shoot hoops with Kee Richard, even though he was extremely clumsy, with a barrel stomach that protruded at least four inches over his belt line. He was a sight to see shooting baskets with shoulder-length hair flying in all directions, missing teeth producing gaping holes when he grinned, long thin arms and legs and of course his huge belly. He dressed in tight jeans, dirty t-shirts and cowboy boots. He grinned when he made his shot as well as when he missed.

Late that summer in early August, Mark Miller returned to the reservation from his vacation with his relatives in Ohio. He had a plan. He decided he would visit some of the boys from the school as they lived with their families. How long he would visit each family would depend on how comfortable he felt. He knew that he might be driving many hours to some far-off canyon for a mere ten-minute visit. He thought it was worth the trouble. It gave him an excuse to see more of the countryside and more importantly, he simply could not continue to teach having so little knowledge of Navajo life.

Mark Miller had been driving through the reservation for a week and a half visiting and sightseeing. He had visited ten families. His visits had lasted as little as five minutes and as long as five hours. The Navajo were as varied in their hospitality as any peoples. When he approached the more traditional families a barking dog usually greeted him and then perhaps one person would show himself and speak a neutral "yah-ta-eh." Others, in sight, would go about their business. Children sometimes hid behind rocks. The boy he was looking for was always off herding sheep. More progressive Navajos would sit him down to a cup of coffee and even share a meal. They seem to enjoy the sitting and talking even though at times conversation lagged. These Navajos could usually find the boy for whom Mark was looking and eavesdropped as he and Mark conversed.

Now Mark bumped along the dusty trail in his Jeep to Kee Richard's hogan. He hoped that he was accurately following the directions that he had received from the fellow at the trading post. Kee Richard was the last and most isolated student on his itinerary. As he rumbled up a thirty-degree incline full of ruts and holes, he made a sharp left turn at the top to avoid hitting a clump of cedar. Mark pulled to a quick stop. He was high up overlooking a vast desert scene and straight away in front of him was a four-by-four post with a basketball hoop. A pot-bellied man and a boy were shooting hoops. To his right was a hogan and beyond that a corral full with sheep, and then a hill down to an arroyo. Mark parked his truck just a few feet off the track. Two dogs came barking in his direction. The basketball players stopped, glanced at him and then stared at the ground. No one came from the hogan.

Kee Richard spoke in Navajo to Charlie Pete; "It's Mr. Miller from the boarding school." Neither Charlie nor Kee Richard moved to greet Mark. They looked at the ground and waited. Mark walked within ten feet and gave the familiar "Yah-ta-eh." Charlie worked with Anglos and could fit in. Yet when Anglos came to the hogan, he felt very Navajo. The three stood around the hoop in silence. Mark finally began to talk. He told them that he was visiting students so that he could get to know the Navajo ways. He did not want to be so much a stranger when teaching. He told them that he had heard that traditional Navajo did not like strangers teaching their children and that he did not want to be a stranger. Charlie Pete finally spoke, "Would you like some coffee?" Mark responded with a "No, thank you" and indicated that he had an ice-cold cooler full of soda pop in the jeep. The three sat in silence enjoying the cool liquid as it cleansed the dust from their mouths.

Charlie told Mark that he and Kee Richard had been shooting baskets. Mark did not realize that the two had been shooting around for the past three weeks, whenever they were not herding sheep. Charlie had taken vacation from his job at Navajo Tribal Utility to help Kee Richard with the sheep as the rest of the family traveled to the other side of the reservation to be with some relatives.

Mark placed his can on a rock and said, "Let's shoot some hoops." He picked up the basketball and attempted a twenty-foot jump shot. It hit the rim and bounded high. Mark was quickly under it, grabbed it on the first bounce and laid it into the hoop. Charlie had put down his drink and Mark shot a quick pass to him. Charlie dribbled in ten feet and shot. It bounded to the left. Mark chased it down and took a jumper, which to his embarrassment hit nothing but air—far over the hoop. Mark yelled, "No net, why don't you have a net?" he kidded Charlie. "I need a net for perspective; I can't shoot without one." Charlie smiled, walked over to where the ball lay and carefully fired a set shot. Mark knew that Charlie's shot had gone through the hoop and yet he yelled, "There's no net, and I can't tell if that went through the hoop or was just another air ball." Mark grabbed the ball, bounced it a few times and then shot a pass over to Kee Richard. Kee Richard shot from about twenty-five feet.

Mark wasn't sure this time if the ball had gone through the hoop or was simply a close air ball. He walked over to his jeep and rummaged around some junk in the back and came up with a used, frayed net. He yelled to Charlie, "Do you have a ladder or something I can stand on?" Charlie smiled and walked over to the hoop, said something to Kee Richard in Navajo, bent his knees and braced his upper body with his hands on his quads. Kee Richard took off his boots and climbed onto Charlie's back with one hand on the four-by-four to balance himself. Charlie told Mark to hand the net up to Kee Richard. Kee Richard quickly had the net in place. After that, the three took turns shooting. The same agility Mark observed in Kee Richard on the obstacle course was evident here. He was a natural shooter, rebounder and dribbler. Even without coaching he was as good as most ninth grade players and he had grown taller. Mark estimated that Kee Richard was now about six foot one. Mark knew that most Navajo basketball players were very coachable team players with total court awareness. He thought that if Kee Richard played basketball and grew any taller, he could be a phenomenon on the reservation. Yet, Mark knew that this scenario did not fit with this kid's personality. He would fit in but never be outstanding.

The afternoon passed and the evening chill was upon them. Mark indicated that he must leave. Charlie explained that Kee Richard's parents were away and would not be back for a day or two and that Mark was welcome to spend the night. This was a first for Mark and he readily accepted the invitation. After a meal of canned corned beef hash and stale fry bread washed down with soda pop, the two men and the boy sat by the open fire in silence.

Kee Richard had said very little to Mark. Mark thought he would try to break the silence: "Kee Richard, would you like to play basketball at school?" "I don't know," responded Kee Richard. There was a long silence until Charlie spoke. "The boy is traditional Navajo; it is difficult for him to play white men's games. I know because I did. Navajo like the movement, the harmony of the ball and hoop. White men like to beat on one another and parade around as big shot winners. Navajo like the running, the jumping, the ball and hoop. At a squaw dance there is gambling and races. Somehow it's different than white man's way. Coyote's trickery is always respected by Navajos." Mark indicated to Charlie that he didn't fully understand what Charlie was trying to say.

Charlie Pete had lived in the white man's world enough to understand Mark. Charlie in fact really didn't fully embrace either world. As the conversation between the two men continued Kee Richard listened intently. Both men made sense and he could feel that both were groping for truth, which neither man seemed to have firmly in his grasp. His father and mother had a truth. The Anglo world had a truth. He was a Navajo; he must live the truth of his parents.

Kee Richard finally spoke. "No basketball for me," and left the fire to sleep in the hogan. Mark apologized to Charlie Pete and Charlie apologized to Mark. The two men sat silently listening to the desert night and watching the clear night sky for the truth. A falling star fell through the sky-hoop. Mark took this as a slam-dunk end to the evening. He bid Charlie "good night" and crawled into his sleeping bag.

When Mark awoke, he rolled out of his sleeping bag just in time to watch Kee Richard and Charlie Pete herd the sheep around the hill and out of sight. Mark took a deep breath of the cool fresh morning air, rolled up his bag, settled into the driver's seat of his jeep, thought for a moment of what he had learned the day before and headed for the highway. At the highway he turned right, toward Window Rock. He would rest at Navajo Motor Lodge that night. In the morning he had a nine o'clock appointment with the principal at Window Rock High School in Fort Defiance. He hadn't planned on leaving the boarding school; however the principal at Window Rock had called him on the recommendation of a friend. With more and better roads the boarding school would probably close down within a few years. Window Rock was a much bigger high school with better athletes, better salaries and better equipment. The final reason he was considering a change was a young female teacher whom he had met at a conference and with whom he corresponded all summer.

Three lives had come together—Kee Richard Yazzie, Mark Miller and Charlie Pete. The serendipity of the universe, the whirling hoop of sky dancer, the circle of life and the treachery of Coyote would not allow them to separate. As Mark was signing a contract with Window Rock School District, a tragic event was happening in the life of young Kee Richard. On their return home from their visit with relatives on the very same night that Mark had left the Yazzie hogan, Kee Richard's family pickup truck slammed into a horse wandering across the road. The truck flipped, rolled down a hill and burst into flames. All were killed.

A Navajo tribal policeman drove out to the Yazzie hogan. The owner of the trading post had told him that Kee Richard was there with Charlie Pete. No one knows how devastating the news was to Kee Richard. His grief was silent and alone. Charlie was stunned. At first he had no idea of what to do. In consultation with other relatives, Charlie decided to sell the sheep, give up the grazing ground and take Kee Richard to live with him on the outskirts of Fort Defiance. Within two weeks the family was buried, the sheep sold and Kee Richard moved to Fort Defiance.

Mark didn't like everything about Window Rock High School; however, there were many positives. His nights and weekends were free except for coaching since he had no dormitory to care for. He was much closer to Gallup, Albuquerque and Flagstaff for weekend interests. He liked being close enough to routinely enjoy the company of the young woman he had met the previous year. He was not sure whether he liked the mixture of Anglo and Navajo students. The Anglo kids were only ten percent of the student body and yet they dominated everything. Their parents were doctors, lawyers, teachers and other professionals who worked for the tribe, the BIA or the public health hospital. The Anglo kids traveled all over the United States in the summertime. Generally, they were goal oriented and aggressive. The Navajo kids seemed to be more confused about their identity, caught between two cultures. Tradition was not deeply rooted in them. They were not fluent in either Navajo or English.

Because of this mixture of kids and the greater numbers, Mark saw a distinct difference in the quality of athletes. Generally the Window Rock kids were stronger and more skilled. Of course the Anglos were very much focused and goal oriented. As the head basketball and track coach he could field very competitive teams. Of course the competition would be tougher when they played non-reservation schools. Preliminary workouts with his varsity basketball team indicated that they would be small, quick, and skilled. His point guard would probably be a white boy, the son of a fellow teacher whose father had taught him the game since he could first walk—a kid who had gone to basketball camp in the big cities every summer and who had watched many college and pro games. His other guard was a small

Navajo kid who could shoot and dribble fairly well. However, that was all he could do. His forwards were also Navajo who played a good passing game and average defense. His center was a big six-foot-seven-inch white kid with little talent; he had to play him to match up with off-reservation teams if they were to get any rebounds.

His bench players were small, fast, mediocre players. No one on his bench was an aggressive defensive player. Mark was a good coach and developed an offense and defense that most suited the composition of his team. The Navajos were not aggressive enough; the white point guard tried to do everything himself and the big center was too clumsy to be effective at anything except rebounding.

Kee Richard disliked Window Rock High School as much as the boarding school. Living with Uncle Charlie Pete was okay although he did not feel at home in a wood frame, four-cornered prefab Anglo house. Kee Richard had brought very little with him from the hogan. The sudden death of his entire family seemed to leave him empty, dazed, listless and withdrawn. Charlie tried to be a good uncle; however, he did not know what to say or do when Kee Richard refused to go to school. Kee Richard walked alone in the hills while other kids were in school and Charlie at work. Sometimes he would take Charlie's wine or beer and get drunk. It was for this very reason that Charlie brought back the hoop from the Yazzie family hogan. Every day after work Kee Richard and Charlie played basketball.

One day a tribal social worker came to Charlie's place to inquire as to why the boy had not attended school. She told Charlie that the boy must attend school or she would see that he was taken from Charlie and placed with a family. Kee Richard decided right then and there that he would attend school. Charlie Pete asked the social worker, Rita Nez, if he could arrange for a Blessing Way ceremony for Kee Richard before he attended school. This would delay school for a few more weeks. Herself Navajo, the social worker agreed.

The very next week Charlie Pete bumped into Mark Miller at the large general store in Window Rock. Mark was surprised to learn that Kee Richard was living with Charlie just as Charlie was surprised to find that Mark was teaching and coaching at Window Rock School. Charlie told Mark everything that happened and then invited him to the Blessing Way ceremony.

Mark was delighted. This was the first opportunity to attend a ceremony. Charlie had invited Mark for several reasons. First, it was the polite thing to do; secondly, he liked Mark. Thirdly, Mark was one of the few white men that had gone out of his way to attempt to understand the Navajo way. Finally, he thought that Mark might be helpful to Kee Richard when he began school.

Two weeks later the ceremony was held at Steamboat. Mark arrived on the final afternoon of the ceremony. The singing, the sand painting, the open fire, the roasting mutton, the men dancing and in the evening the clear star-filled night sky removed Mark from any reality he had ever known and placed him in communion with Father Sky, Mother Earth, the Navajo way, Charlie Pete and Kee Richard Yazzie. He didn't understand it; he simply felt it.

On a Sunday night, the night before Kee Richard was to begin school, Mark unexpectedly arrived at Charlie Pete's home. He thanked Charlie for having invited him to the ceremony and asked if he and Kee Richard would accompany him a short distance up Coyote Canyon for a surprise he had prepared for them.

Mark drove Charlie and Kee Richard up the small canyon, stopping at a clearing surrounded by twisted cedar. The night was dark there except for the light of Mark's lantern. Mark immediately lit a small fire that he had prepared earlier. The three sat around the fire and Mark began to explain. Mark had been so inspired by the Blessing Way Ceremony that he felt he needed to prepare a small ceremony of his own to help Kee Richard in school. He told them that he wanted Kee Richard to do well in school and that he would be willing to help him. He also indicated that he wanted Kee Richard to play basketball for the school team. He told Kee Richard and Charlie that basketball was a dance—a harmony of team members, ball and hoop. A ritual dance of battle between good and evil, a dance of the hunter and the hunted, a dance that comes to a climax as the ball falls through the hoop. At that moment, the whole world is in balance—all is correct. Furthermore, each time the ball falls through the hoop there is a new beginning, a new challenge, a renewed attempt to remain centered as your enemies attempt to overpower you. The basketball dance was a ritual like unto life itself and that if one did not understand this ritual in terms of one's own life, it was simply a senseless game.

Mark led Kee Richard and Charlie by lantern away from the fire and showed a sand painting he had created that day. Mark had bought a bag of clean play sand and mixed portions of it with food coloring. Grabbing handfuls of the colorful sand, Mark had formed designs on the earth in imitation of the medicine man at the Blessing Way ceremony. Mark formed a four-foot diameter circle into four areas—the four corners of the earth, the four directions, the four sacred mountains. One section had a crudely drawn picture of a thunderbird, the spirit of the life, wisdom and power. Another had a drawing of a book, the white man's knowledge. The third had a drawing of Father Sky with stars falling through a hoop. The fourth contained a drawing of the Window Rock; a large naturally formed round hole, a window, eroded through solid rock, which gave the area its name.

Mark asked Kee Richard to sit in the middle of the sand and as in all ceremonies the colorful sand mixed into an abstract design as Kee Richard walked into the middle and sat down. Mark asked Charlie to sing as he recited the twenty-third psalm. Mark ended the ceremony with the serenity prayer, "God grant me the serenity to accept the things I cannot change... The courage to change the things I can...and the wisdom to know the difference." In silence the men drove back to Charlie's house and in silence they separated.

The next time Mark saw Kee Richard was in his gym class. Kee Richard was the six-foot-four silent new kid in school whom everyone was talking about but with whom no one could talk. In public Mark treated Kee Richard as if he had not known him previously. Anything else would be embarrassing to Kee Richard. There was one big difference in Kee Richard. He was playing in a pick-up basketball game at the far end of the court and was dazzling everyone with his height and his offensive skills. His individual skills were good enough to place him on the varsity team immediately; however, he knew nothing about the team game and played as if he were the only one on the court.

During the week, Kee Richard's play had become the talk of the school. Kee Richard, silent and shy, seemed oblivious to the talk and simply went on his own way. Students asked Coach Mark if he had recruited the new kid to help the team. Teachers had heard the gossip and were also asking questions. Mark refused to explain anything. He soon occupied his classes in conditioning activities and other games. Kee Richard participated minimally. Mark said nothing more to Kee Richard about playing basketball and Kee Richard did not try out for the team. Mark did notice however that Charlie Pete brought Kee Richard to every home game.

One Wednesday afternoon Kee Richard appeared at Mark's coaching office. He told Mark that he was not doing well in school and that he understood very little. He reminded Mark that he had promised to help him. From then on, two days a week, Kee Richard came to Mark's office and did his schoolwork while Mark coached. After practice, Mark went over Kee Richard's work and explained those things that he obviously did not understand. Kee Richard began to do well as a student. However, whenever a teacher praised him in front of others, he turned away. In fact he had been punished several times for walking out of class while the teacher was speaking to him.

The next school year when Kee Richard was in tenth grade, he began his basketball career at Window Rock High School under Coach Mark Miller. In fact in his three years of playing basketball there, Kee Richard broke school records in points scored and steals. He was a phenomenon not only on the reservation but also within the whole state of Arizona. In his junior year, the Window Rock Scouts won the state championship for the very first time and then duplicated the achievement in his senior year. Kee Richard was a second team high school all-American.

Many colleges from the Southwest sought after Kee Richard. He chose to attend Arizona State University in Tempe. He had no goals. He did not have a clear reason to attend college. Why was he there? What courses should he take? In high school he had Mark Miller to help him through his studies and Charlie Pete to encourage him when life was hard. At the university, no one cared as long as he played basketball well, and everyone assumed he was happy with the situation. Kee Richard had grown to love the game of basketball; however he believed it was a ritual that somehow must be played off the court, played out in the life that surrounds you. This is what confused Kee Richard. He had no purpose to his life in the Anglo world. Herding sheep in the mountains made more sense to him than driving a sports car through the city.

Kee Richard was a pleasure for a coach to have on a team. He spoke little, listened and executed. He had the talent and the discipline to carry out the coach's instructions. As a freshman at Arizona State, Kee Richard became a public hero. Because he was a full-blooded Navajo, the local newspaper crowned him "The Chief of Hoops." Before games the fans would chant "Chief, Chief, Chief, Chief of Hoops" over and over again and again.

Mark was busy teaching, coaching and paying attention to his new bride, Theresa. Charlie Pete visited Kee Richard as often as possible. Charlie recognized that something was wrong with Kee Richard. The busy university life, the struggle in classes for good grades, the constant attention by fans and the press were taking their toll on the Low Mountain Indian kid.
After the final game of Kee Richard's freshman year, after Kee Richard had broken all school scoring records for a first year player, Charlie Pete took Kee Richard out for a late supper. At this dinner Kee Richard confided in Charlie Pete that, like his grandfather during WWII, he had joined the marines to fight in Vietnam. He had seen the recruiter and signed the paper that morning. He was dropping out of school at the end of the quarter. Vietnam would give purpose to his life. He wanted to continue the tradition of loyal Navajo men to the United States of America. Vietnam was another hoop to fall through. If he succeeded he would come back to the reservation.

Charlie could say nothing. He understood the misery of the young man. Charlie's own years of living between two worlds had provided him with little wisdom or advice.

A year after Kee Richard entered the Marines, Mark Miller and his wife departed the reservation because of Theresa's ill health. They returned to Indiana to be nearer to Theresa's family. Mark had written Charlie Pete a few times and tried to obtain Kee Richard's address. Mark never heard from either of them.

Now, eight years later, Mark, his wife, and their two children returned for a visit to the reservation. Of course there had been great changes—more roads, more housing, more commercial buildings, more fences, and more people. Most of the teachers with whom Mark and Theresa had worked had moved back to wherever they had come from. Window Rock, Black Rock and the surrounding red rocks were familiar; they were permanent while everything else had changed.

Mark wondered if Charlie Pete still lived in a mobile home on the outskirts of Fort Defiance. He left his wife and kids at the hotel swimming pool to find Charlie Pete. As Mark pulled up, Charlie was getting into a new pickup truck to drive to Albuquerque for his boss. The two men shook hands and wide grins lit up their faces. Neither had forgotten that they had shared some good moments together. Charlie Pete indicated that he had to leave immediately but that he would return in two days. Mark asked about Kee Richard. Charlie briefly explained that Kee Richard, now twenty-seven years old, was in Fort Defiance Public Health Hospital. He was dying of alcoholism. Charlie said that he had just come from the hospital and would be visiting there again soon as he returned. Tears welled up in Charlie Pete's eyes. He turned from Mark, walked to his truck and drove off.

Mark returned to the hotel and told his wife about Kee Richard. He then drove to the new shopping mall, the first on the reservation, and bought a piece of poster board and some colorful marking pens. Back at the motel room he drew a replica of the sand painting he had created to help Kee Richard adapt to attending Window Rock High School and playing basketball there. He kissed Theresa goodbye and headed for the hospital.

"Ya-ta-eh, my friend," was Mark's greeting as he entered the small gloomy room. The man in the bed turned toward him. He did not look anything like the boy Mark had known. He was so thin and pale in the bed that he looked more like five-foot-seven than six-foot-seven. Mark thought that if Kee Richard stood up and held a basketball he might recognize him. Closer to the bed, Mark could see the yellow jaundice of Kee Richard's skin and eyes. Kee Richard had straggly chin whiskers and his hair was long, oily, and unkempt. If Mark had not known him as a young man, he would have seen him as an old Navajo drunk, a stranger dying of a reservation disease.

A delicate smile came across Kee Richard's face and his eyes brightened as he recognized Mark. Mark held up his drawing and Kee Richard began a barely audible chant as Mark recited the Twenty-third Psalm. Mark placed the drawing on Kee Richard's chest and the two men sat in silence.

Kee Richard began to speak with great labor, "Coach, I jumped through the hoop in high school, I jumped through the hoop in college, I jumped through the hoop in 'Nam, and I am ready to jump through the hoop of death. I'm ready coach, I'm ready to jump.

"I knew I had the taste for liquor as a kid when I first tried it at ceremonies and squaw dances, but I didn't drink in high school, I didn't drink in college, and I didn't drink in 'Nam. I lived the legend of the hoop in those places. After 'Nam, when I came back to the reservation, I felt deeply sorry for my people. They lived between two worlds. I wanted to help them. All I could do to comfort them was to drink with them."

A nurse entered the room, indicating that visiting hours were over and Mark had to leave. The two men faced one another. Kee Richard, with great effort, extended his hand. The two men clasped hands and looked one another in the eyes. Mark turned and left the room.

The next morning Mark phoned Kee Richard. A nurse answered the phone. She said Kee Richard was no longer there; he had died during the night.

Kee Richard Yazzie, like Charlie Pete, had never married. In the last year of his life he gave up drinking and moved in with a Navajo nurse. He lived with her until he moved into the hospital for his last week. Kee Richard's friend, Susie Begay, was a woman of great maturity. She had the practical problem-solving attitude of an Anglo combined with a great sensitivity toward traditional Navajo ways. She was the perfect person to help Kee Richard live his last days in happiness. Mark met her briefly at the grave. He told her who he was and how much he respected her man. She thanked him and their meeting was over.

Charlie and Mark walked back to the van where Theresa had waited with the children. Theresa expressed her condolences to Charlie and then feeling his and Mark's sadness, began to cry.

Charlie tried to explain, "Kee Richard, like many Navajo men, found the peace of the desert and the dreams of their ancestors in a bottle."

Mark left the reservation and never returned. Charlie Pete died of a heart attack six months later. Susie Begay gave birth to Kee Richard's child. Kee Richard Jr. is studying pre-law at the University of New Mexico. From childhood, Kee Richard Yazzie Jr. was told the story of his father by his mother. The Anglos called him the "Chief of Hoops." She reminded her son that the Navajo have no chiefs.

St. John's Eve

A Christmas story with a trilogy

Who asked for this story?

I don't know.

From where did this story come?

I don't know.

For whom is this story written?

I don't know.

Why does this story exist?

I might add,

why do I exist

or you, for that matter?

Huddled beneath the warm heavy blanket, protected
from the frosty room, John breathed the chill air,
listened to the windows rattle as the cold wind seeped
through the cracks, watched the shadows dance over the
walls and ceiling as the wind-blown tree branches
swayed and twisted in the light of the street lamp. He
wondered just how long he could remain nestled there
till his radio alarm sounded. Would the music he awoke
to today be soft, pleasant and cheerful or hard, heavy

and caustic? If the former he would lay there awhile longer, if the latter he would immediately shut it off.

For John, the deliciously peaceful half-sleep was disturbed by distorted images of people and places, incongruent scenarios and irritating thoughts that cluttered his early-morning mind with chaos and anxiety. He broke through this half-awake nightmare by remembering his childhood when at this time of morning the house was already beginning to warm from the freshly stoked coal furnace. His mother was sipping a fresh cup of coffee; his brother was delivering newspapers; his sister was primping for school in the bathroom; his dad was outside warming the car up and shoveling snow from the driveway.

Instead of waiting for the radio to surprise him, John reached over and turned off the timing switch. He pulled back the covers, threw his legs over the side of the bed and sat up. Then, as always, the words came through him. He knew not why. He knew not to whom these words were addressed. He felt the words well up from deep within his tired body, tired mind and errant soul. "Please. Help me through this day."

When John was a boy he had spoken these words to God. Now they were spoken into an empty space within him. The words were melded into his personality and echoed in his personal silence. The echo itself was enough reinforcement to help him face another day.

"Another day!" He thought for a moment and remembered that this day was Christmas Eve. Tomorrow his little snack shop would be closed and he could lie in bed as long as he would like. John moved from the bed across the room to the thermostat and turned it up just enough to allow the heat to pop on. He shuffled over to the kitchen area and began a fresh brew in his two-cup drip pot. He wandered into the bathroom, produced a healthy bowel movement, washed up, brushed and flossed his teeth and combed his thinning hair. He didn't bother trimming his scraggly beard. He didn't look at himself in the mirror long enough to notice it. He remembered his adolescent days when he showered three times in one day and was constantly combing his hair. Of course in childhood there was the ritual of Saturday night bath and hair scrubbing. Now he showered about twice a week and bathed whenever his back bothered him.

John dressed and then sat sipping his coffee for about twenty minutes, thinking of nothing in particular. He ate a few saltine crackers. He bundled into his heaviest coat and pulled a knit cap over his head and ears, shut the door behind him, walked one flight of stairs to the sidewalk and stepped to the bus stop. Snow was falling heavily and glistened in the streetlight. Trees were delicately laced with white. Tracks of a few early morning vehicles unintentionally traced artistic patterns in the snow. In the early morning darkness the forms of the world were highlighted in white. John mused about the mystery of this beauty that distracted him from the cold while waiting for the bus, snow falling on good ruin. The bus ground to a halt, the doors folded back. John stepped up, greeted the bus driver, deposited his coins and found an empty seat by the window near the middle of the bus. Soon the bus would be standing room only. When the bus stopped next, John watched a lady with two canes awkwardly climb the few steps to enter the bus. There was a seat up front for her. Her one leg had a metal brace. She looked worn, thin, cold and without adequate clothing for this kind of weather. Her face and hands had sores on them. John found himself willing this woman all the energy, the life, the warmth that he possessed, as little as it was. She held his attention for only a few moments, yet John had given her all that he could.

Every morning three ladies entered the bus from different stops. They sat up front and engaged in lively conversation. They obviously did not know each other or see one another except for this thirty-minute ride. On this day each had a small gift for the other, which they opened and enjoyed immediately. John thought that these lovely ladies had a remarkable relationship and felt envious of them. They were warm, friendly, fun loving, tender, spontaneous, uninhibited women. They were all that John was not.

The usual crowd was on the bus this morning minus a few who obviously had stayed home to prepare for Christmas festivities. John's own festivities would include a prepared turkey dinner from the supermarket, a bottle of good Merlot wine, a small pumpkin pie with whipped cream and a few old Christmas movies. He especially liked "It's a Wonderful Life," "Miracle on 14th Street," and "Meet John Doe." Someone whom John had not seen before entered the bus, a very young undernourished woman looking very sick and minding a toddler. She was much too young to look so wasted. John watched her carefully and wished he could do something to change her troubled life.

John wedged himself deep into the corner of the seat and stared out the window at the whirling mixture of cars, people, light and falling snow. John thought of the days when he lived on the West Coast and drove a car to work across the Bay Bridge every day. He thought about his many cross-country drives to visit friends through Kansas without speed limits, through mountains and deserts and along the seashore. That was freedom compared to this daily bus ritual. The seat next to John remained open. John often wondered why the seat next to him was most often the last one filled. Did he look that bad? Did he smell? Maybe he created some sort of aura that people stayed clear of?

John buttoned up his coat, pulled his cap on tight and readied himself to depart the bus.

John walked past the panhandler who was just getting up from beneath the cardboard and rags under which he slept on the warm grate. The police didn't bother the sleeping vagrants at night but in the morning they quickly hurried them away from the business area. John had the urge to give this bum everything he owned, everything in the snack shop. He couldn't do that; he couldn't trade places with the man. Because he couldn't give everything, he was too ashamed to give anything. It was a bitter decision. Beggars were a direct link to God; they would always be there to test you, to discover whether you really had offered your life to God. Would you give and not count the cost? Would you give without expecting return? Could you love your neighbor as yourself without conditions? Yeah, that is what life is all about and John knew that he had failed in this quest. Consequently, God had become silent and invisible.

John greeted the security guard as he entered the arcade and headed to the far end towards his little snack shop. The security guard was short and extremely obese. Although a fairly young man he was obviously a good candidate for a massive heart attack. Yet, John admired the man. He was there every day smiling, giving people directions and, like St. Nick, chatting with everyone in a jolly way. John simply hoped the man would never have to handle an emergency. John was afraid that any great amount of exertion would be too much for the man.

John unlocked the large chain-link gate that protected his snack shop and swung it out of the way. He hit the light switch, took a packet of change from his pocket and distributed it into his small cash drawer, hung up his coat and cap, filled a large coffee urn with water from the sink, plopped a pre-measured sack of coffee in the receptacle, set the brewing device, opened a bundle of newspapers, placed one half on the counter, checked the shelves for candy, cigarettes, cookies and other snack items, added a few bottles of spring water to the cooler and finally sat down on his stool to rest and allow his eyes and mind to relax. At this early hour, only a few people from the night cleaning shift would stop on their way out. He came early for them and himself. These early morning quiet hours allowed his mind to wander.

Normally John could allow his eyes to gaze down the long corridor of the arcade. However, the arcade management had placed a life-size Christmas manger scene just twelve steps in front of his snack shop in the middle of the corridor. Actually it was the only space in the arcade big enough to allow pedestrian traffic around the manger. It blocked his view and John had to be content with studying this scene—the mother, the father, the baby, the shepherds, kings, animals and trees.

As often it did, John's mind took on a life of its own. At times he seemed to enter into other people's lives. People and places of which he had no familiarity became alive and familiar. If people knew this, some would think him loony. Others might think he was a terrific daydreamer. Others might say he is experiencing past life. Maybe he connected at these times into the collective unconscious or perhaps he was mentally ill. John had no idea which explanation was correct. All he knew was that he would enter without effort into a life story, beginning, middle and end.

This morning a shepherd in the manger scene would bring about this reality:

The Shepherd

*A vision has no name and
prophecy is humbled by language.
Humans speak as they have been taught and
their God has many names.
Behold, God is both Father and Mother
of "All-that-is."*

Son-Ali felt the warmth of Sun-King as the first golden streaks of Sun-King's glowing arms pierced Ghost-Mist and chased Shadow from Dawn. The bright dayflower revealed "What-He-Could-See" and Night Father uncoupled from Earth-Mother. Rolling from his sleep-skin, Son-Ali stood tall facing Sun-King and chanted his welcome song. Son-Ali's bones would not ache from the cold as he walked the mountain path on this day. His feet stamped dusty Earth-Mother three times, right-left-right, and thanked her for being there for him. Son-Ali shuffled over to a small pile of stones near the cedar branches, which boxed his sheep into the end of the canyon. One by one, he picked stones from the pile, massaged and examined each, held each up to Sun-King, rubbed each on the grit of Earth-Mother and began to stack them anew. He set each in place with enough force to cause a stone against stone click to echo through the small canyon and reveal his presence to Day-Spirits who would bless him for his care of "All-That-He-Could-See."

Son-Ali's sheep would be led by the Day-Spirits to fresh grass and cool water. Son-Ali rarely needed to do anything except follow the sheep. Occasionally Day-Woman or Night-Father might call upon him to protect his sheep. In these emergencies, he relied on his ancestral spirits to possess him. Their skill and courage would be his own.

Son-Ali's life was a perpetual "Thank you" to all the spirits and to "All-That-Is."

For two days now, the Day-Spirits had been leading Son-Ali into the face of Sun-King. The path led out of his own desert territory, over the mountain and into the hill country of Judea and towards the friendly Hebrew herdsmen who lived there. The hills of Judea and the trek that had brought Son-Ali there were seldom used by his people except in the driest of seasons. The Day-Spirits knew the dryness of his own land and the need his sheep had for good water and grass. Son-Ali thanked the Day-Spirits and he thanked "All-That-Is."

When Son-Ali's sheep entered a canyon where Water-Spirit had cracked solid rock to allow fresh water to flow into pools and bring moisture to grasses and trees, Son-Ali knew that Earth-Mother had gifts even in the driest of seasons. This place would be theirs to feed upon till seasons changed and Sky-Father entertained Changing-Light, Rain-Warrior, and Snow-Woman.

Son-Ali had camped alone in the canyon for almost one turn of Moon-Woman when Hebrew herdsmen began to arrive with their sheep. At evening fires, the Hebrew herdsmen told stories, sang and danced. Most of their lore concerned their God, Jehovah, and the promise of a savior who was to come soon. Son-Ali understood only a little of their language and yet the friendly Hebrews welcomed him to their fires. He spoke very little and yet listened intently. As he understood, the Hebrew's Jehovah was "All-That-Is" and the savior was a new Earth-Sky spirit who would guide the people along good paths.

The full face of Moon-Woman had come and gone twice since Son-Ali and the other shepherds had come to that canyon. Grass was becoming scarce, and Rain-Warrior sent chilly Cold-Child to Night-Father. On occasion, Rain-

Warrior danced in the canyon, warning Son-Ali that his storms would soon come to the mountains to cleanse the way for mountain Snow-Woman. Son-Ali knew that he must not linger too long in that place; he knew that he must leave this hill country soon if he wished to travel safely over the mountains to his own country and his own people.

During the final month of Son-Ali's visit to the canyon, increasing numbers of strangers on their way to nearby towns to fulfill their duty to the Roman rulers wandered through the countryside. The Romans had decreed that every man return to his ancestral home with his family in order to be counted in the census. Son-Ali's tribe lived in inhospitable land far from settlements, and had no fear of Romans. They did not participate in these Roman laws. Romans did not bother such poor people living in such desolate places.

Son-Ali noticed that Night-Sky-Father was acting strangely. Over the past few days, a new form was taking shape among the Sky-Spirits, and Moving-Light-Spirit rushed across the face of Sky-Father. The Hebrew shepherds did not know what to think of it, unless it was a sign from Jehovah. Son-Ali danced and sang around his night fire and shouted to Sky-Father to protect them from this new spirit. Even the Hebrew shepherds with their faith in Jehovah were frightened. Son-Ali listened to the psalms of the Hebrews and yet he himself preferred to appeal to "All-That-He-Could-See" and "All-That-Is."

On the evening before Son-Ali was to depart the canyon for his own country, a man and his wife entered the canyon and took shelter in one of the small caves near the far end. The young woman was about to give birth.

That night, Son-Ali sang to Sky-Father and the new Sky-Spirit with such intensity that he seemed to be one with the spirit world. The new Sky-Spirit stretched a long arm towards the canyon and Son-Ali climbed that arm to see Earth-Mother as Sky-Father saw her. He recognized his own tent on the other side of the mountain range and within he saw his wife peacefully sleeping. He saw a large group of travelers sleeping in the streets of the overcrowded small town near the canyon. He saw evil night spirits fleeing across the desert and into the mountains. Finally, he saw into the canyon where his own body lay, where the herdsmen and their sheep slept, where the stranger and his pregnant wife had taken shelter. Son-Ali saw the birth in the cave and heard the infant cry. The cry echoed off the canyon walls and gently awakened the hills to new life. Gentle Day-Spirits awoke in the night, jumped from trees, rose up out of the tall grass and water pools, stepped from large boulders and danced a joyful dance for "All-That-Is."

Son-Ali knew that the new Night-Spirit was a Light-Spirit that allowed Day-Spirits to dance in darkness. This new Light-Spirit, however, was no longer in the sky. The light now emanated from the cave, from the newborn infant. The infant was the Light-Spirit who would shine on all people of all tribes, uniting them into the dance of light. Son-Ali's understanding of "All-That-He Could-See" united with the Hebrew Jehovah, the one God, the God whom he called "All-That-Is."

Suddenly, Son-Ali's spirit re-entered his body. He sprang up and began to dance. He shouted to the other shepherds to awaken and sing their praises to Jehovah, for the infant within the cave was the Messiah they had been awaiting.

The shepherds, who normally sleep lightly in their concern for danger, awoke alert and ready for any threat that might befall them.

The shepherds had seen people possessed by evil spirits, people with false as well as true visions, people who were false prophets as well as true prophets. They studied the night air. They looked deeply within their own hearts and listened to Son-Ali. They felt their bodies tingle with excitement and felt the warm glow of Jehovah's love for them. While Son-Ali thanked "Sky-Father," "Earth-Mother," and "All-That-Is" for this new "Man-Child-Light-Spirit," the Hebrews praised Jehovah for the infant-Messiah.

"John, John, wake up. I'll have a newspaper and a cup of coffee. Here is a five-dollar bill. Keep it all, and Merry Christmas."

Awakened from his dream, John was soon busy in the midst of people coming and going from the arcade. The hustle and bustle made the time pass quickly and it was almost noon when Mr. Simon of "Simon, Simon & Simon," the law office on the third floor, came up to the snack shop for a candy bar.

"Merry Christmas, John, and here is a bottle of very excellent liqueur for you to sip on over the holidays. I just wanted to let you know how much we appreciate your being here for us. I'm headed home early today and won't be back till after New Year's. Happy New Year."

Traffic in the arcade was slowing down. This was a business arcade and most businesses were closing early for Christmas Eve. John decided to stick around for one more hour and then close up shop. He looked across the way at the manger. This time, the three kings dressed in splendor, with heavily laden camels, attracted his attention. One king looked like a bear with a grumpy disposition; another looked soft and simple, with a broad smile. The third king's eyes were dilated and intently staring at the manger as if seeing beyond the present.

Kings

My body withers. My knees bend and unbend with great effort. My left shoulder aches. Pus oozes from my gums. Weak lungs rasp with each struggle for breath. I relax and extend my awareness to the world outside my body, outside the present tense to the stories of the past, which portend what is yet to come.

I am the last to have personally known the great King Melchior or should I say now, the great lover Melchior, the great wise man Melchior. Melchior, who died imprisoned by his own son, would not lift a hand in his own defense. I was ordered to minister to his needs and for ten years he remained, as ordered, within the confines of this garden.

During Melchior's time with me, he told many stories and helped me understand the journey he had taken, and how it changed his world. He spoke to me about an Earth that could not possibly be cow dung on the back of a turtle. He spoke of other kings he had befriended and of their adventures together. He spoke of the birth of a child and the understanding among friends that brought him and his friends to the child. He spoke of the bond of love between all men and women. He spoke of the nourishing mother, Earth, and her entire people. He often said that we played the chess game on a flat board because we do not understand that existence is a sphere and that which is within the sphere and around the sphere are as important as the surface of the sphere. The within and the without is the balance which causes chaos or harmony on the surface.

Now, old man that I am, unwanted as I am, alone as I am, I write these scriptures for someone to find and be enlightened by the wisdom that found King Melchior.

In as much as Melchior told his stories absentmindedly in fits and spasms of memory, I will attempt to make sense of them at the risk of losing some detail as well as spontaneity.

Melchior's story began with sleepless nights, fitful dreaming and a change in alignment of the stars. The sleepless nights tired him. Exhaustion led to indecision over the affairs of the kingdom and then angry retaliation when nothing was done about the problems. When he could sleep, the dreaming caused him great anxiety over his own imperfections, which as a king he was not allowed to admit. The dreams tormented him with his own weaknesses and mortality. The new alignment of the stars was his only escape as he consulted his astrologers as to the meaning of life and the future of his own life.

As his kingdom became more chaotic, Melchior spent more and more of his time gazing at the stars. He had become convinced that the new alignment was for him alone. He came to the conclusion that he would never be happy unless he traveled in the direction to which the stars pointed. His sanity as well as his life depended upon finding the source of life.

One night Melchior gave the symbols of power to his son and secretly left his kingdom with six of his most trusted guards. Even though his astrologers had warned him that it would take hundreds of dangerous days to reach the source, he was determined to move swiftly and unnoticed through whatever environment, whatever kingdom, whatever disaster lie between himself and the source.

Once into the journey, indecision and anxiety were left behind. At night he slept peacefully under the stars. He and his men began to look like poor wanderers and yet his spirit was more kingly than ever.

King Melchior had learned quickly that kingliness was not born unto or bestowed upon a person. Melchior learned while traveling with his men through the mountains that a king had to be free of interior bondage in order to act as a king should. He was now free to be spontaneous, creative and excited by a goal in a way he could never have been while confined by the politics and ritual of his kingdom.

Melchior and his men had traveled for almost thirty days through the mountains without incident. Now standing at the edge of the desert, each knew that this unfamiliar land would test them. Each night in the mountains Melchior had gazed at the stars and shared with his men the purpose of the journey. He promised that when found, each would share in the reward. Thus, no one looked back as they exchanged their tired mountain ponies for camels and trekked out onto the blistering sands of the vast desert.

Abdah, a camel boy who tended the six pack-camels, had been sold to Melchior for the journey. If he were returned in good health at the end of the journey, he would be sold back to his original owner. Melchior knew that Abdah was important to the success of the journey since his knowledge of the desert and of camels far exceeded that of Melchior and his men. Melchior, who had never felt dependent on anyone as he sat on his throne protected by the ritual of his kingdom, now began to understand that he was dependent on his men as well as the young camel boy.

One evening well into the journey, Melchior sat atop a high sand dune and as usual was stargazing. There was no magic that he knew of that could bring a forest of wood here to build shelter or a fire on this cold desert night. There was no magic that he knew of that could produce the cold mountain snow to cool the heat of the day. The living Earth had its time and place. He mused that this life is a balance of cold and heat, desert and mountain, water and soil, male and female, night and day, king and subject which somehow penetrate and balance each other to maintain life.

Melchior's thoughts were interrupted by the awareness that his two advance scouts had not returned. As was the rule they were to ride ahead till just past mid-day and then return to the camp at dusk. The sun had set many hours ago. The scouts may not have been able to find the camp or perhaps they ran into trouble. Melchior could not sleep. Abdah came to him and asked, "Why does a king worry about two of his subjects?" Melchior did not answer because he knew his own worry was a true concern for those two men—concern for their hopes, their dreams, their love of life—not just his own ambition, but theirs. A king could not say this to a camel boy.

The braying of the camels and the shouts of men awoke Melchior from his thoughts. The sun was already above the horizon—past time to break camp. One of the scouts had returned with news of a small army of over two hundred soldiers camped at a great river not far from where they were. The scouts had been captured by a patrol from the army of two great kings. They held one wounded scout and sent the other back to ask Melchior to declare his intentions or proceed no further. The scout indicated that the army did not know where Melchior was camped and that he was sure he had not been followed.

The two great kings had no information about Melchior and had already begun to set up defensive positions as if Melchior might have an army. Melchior thought, "Good, let them think we have an army while we decide what to do." Now, for the first time, Melchior consulted the five remaining soldiers. Abdah was not included and had become curious about the two great kings and slipped away to see them for himself.

Melchior discussed the options with his men. They could simply wait till the army moved. However, this may be too long a time and a patrol may discover their camp. Perhaps the captured soldier would be tortured into telling who, how many, and where they were, and where they were going. Waiting did not seem like a good idea. They could move around the army and find a place to cross the river at a considerable distance from it. Melchior and his men agreed that they could wait one day while scouting the river for a safe place to cross. Perhaps in this time the army of the two great kings would have moved on. An army of two hundred was small, especially for two kings. They must also be in a hurry to arrive somewhere. They may be on a quick and ruthless war pilgrimage. If this were so they would show no mercy to King Melchior and his men.

Curious, Abdah cautiously guided his camel around, but never over the sand dunes. He did not wish to be seen by a patrol of the two great kings and be killed even before he had a chance to speak. Abdah liked King Melchior, and yet like others of his trade, had no particular loyalty to him. His father and his father's father had been sold to caravans criss-crossing the desert. Although only seventeen years of age, Abdah could speak three languages fluently, and six others sufficiently. He felt confident that these two great kings would speak one of these languages and he could find out news of the desert. He could possibly help King Melchior; or, on the other hand, he could sell himself to these great kings who may be able to provide better for him. Abdah's plan was to simply ride directly into the large encampment. He knew whereas a patrol might kill him instantly, the large encampment would not feel threatened by one camel boy.

Just as Abdah thought, the soldiers were not particularly belligerent as he rode from behind a dune into full sight of the camp. He was immediately surrounded by approximately fifteen horsemen. Obviously they had been watching him pick his way through the dunes for some time. Also as he expected, they spoke a language with which he was somewhat familiar, just as Melchior's had been. The men who captured Abdah were obviously relaxed. They laughed and talked to themselves even as they questioned Abdah. They took him to an officer who offered Abdah food, water and conversation. The officer acted as if Abdah were only a wandering camel boy, while believing that he was perhaps a spy for whomever's army followed them. The other scout had died of his wounds and was not able to give any information.

Because of the relaxed manner of the situation, knowing that Melchior was no match for such an army, and having no loyalties, Abdah offered all that he knew about Melchior and his men. He told the officer about the search for an event connected to the source of life and that Melchior was reading the stars.

As Abdah sat in relaxed conversation, fifty men mounted horses to capture Melchior. The capture was easy inasmuch as Melchior ordered his men to put down their arms and leave themselves at the mercy of the captors. The languages were dissimilar and there was no communication as Melchior and his men were escorted to the camp of the two great kings. Although kingly in demeanor, Melchior looked more like a wanderer than a king. The general who stood before Melchior sensed that

there was more to the man than was seen. He called for
Abdah to interpret for them and asked Melchior to sit and
talk of his intentions. Now Melchior was faced with a
choice. Does he reveal his kingship and his destination or
does he conceal this? He reasoned that if Abdah told them
where he was, he also told all else. He answered, "I am
King Melchior and I travel to the source of life as told by
the stars."

The two great kings sat in a tent somewhat removed from
where the general and King Melchior sat, and yet were
kept informed of all that was said.

King Balthazar from the north was a totally autocratic
and demanding ruler. His astronomers had told him of a
great event as foretold in the stars, and his only
motivation for his journey was the pride of being there for
whatever was to happen. Everyone approached this man
with fear except King Gaspar, a weak person, a weak
ruler, a young buffoon who inherited a kingdom before he
grew up. However, King Gaspar could make King
Balthazar laugh. Balthazar had conquered this young
king and yet kept him in power simply because it was his
whim. Actually, Balthazar believed there was only one
great king and that was himself.

At first Balthazar was alarmed that Melchior had called
himself a king. However, he realized that a man with only
six guards and a disloyal camel boy, and dressed like a
beggar couldn't be much of a king. When he heard of this
so-called king's destination he became thoughtful because
his own destination was the same. This man, if not a king,
was not simply chattel. In fact he may have knowledge
that might be put to his own use.

Thus, at Balthazar's command, the three kings sat
together in the middle of a large open tent—Balthazar
the severe, Gaspar the lighthearted and Melchior the

contemplative. Only Abdah sat with them to act as interpreter.

Balthazar, feeling magnanimous, had decided to entertain Melchior as a fellow king even though he felt that Melchior was no more worthy to be king than was Gaspar. Servants brought food and drink to them quickly and retreated as Balthazar opened the meeting with a toast to Melchior and his faraway kingdom with great emphasis on the "far away." Melchior returned his salute in kind and Gaspar praised the both of them. Gaspar, however, coughed in the midst of drinking and sent a spray of wine over the food, Balthazar and Melchior. Balthazar laughed heartily, and then with Abdah interpreting, got down to business.

Balthazar told Melchior that he was traveling for the same reason as he and that he wished Melchior to travel with him. This was more a command than a request. Balthazar's own astrologers had brought him as far as the river but he was unsure of them. His command-request was for Melchior to lead him the rest of the way.

Melchior reasoned that if this great event were truly the source of all life then there would be enough to share with these two kings. This was an intense personal journey for Melchior and he was not interested in the power he might obtain. Originally, he had thought that the signs were just for him. The long journey had convinced him that there was more life, more variety, more earth than he had ever realized, and that the source must be strong enough to maintain all of it. His concept of deity had changed from the one that had resided on the mountain dominating his valley kingdom. Since leaving his kingdom, wherever he walked he felt life—a vibration under him, a mist surrounding him, a force that emanated from the ground on which he stood. This deity had as its source the place on which the earth rested. Vibrations in the earth were movements of the turtle in reaction to man's actions. The mist as well as rain and fire were the turtle's breath. The turtle could heal or destroy men.

Melchior was not confused as to the direction to which the stars pointed and was willing to lead the two kings there. From this point on the three kings traveled together. Abdah would not be a camel boy any longer. He would be a respected interpreter, constantly at the side of the three kings. Balthazar gave the orders, Gaspar provided amusement, and Melchior read the stars.

Balthazar had already built rafts and found a gentle place to cross the river. His men had scouted the other side and saw no signs of danger. Even though Balthazar had only two hundred warriors, he also had over one hundred craftsmen, servants and herders with sheep, goats, camels, and horses. At sunrise of the third day, the caravan began to cross the river and by nightfall everyone was camped on the other side. Everyone was exhausted and the camp fell quietly to sleep.

Balthazar's scouts had missed seeing eyes and that very night fifty horsemen surprised the troops. The brigands made off with ten pack camels and killed five of Balthazar's men. Balthazar was angry and was about to order one hundred of his men to pursue at sunrise when Gaspar sang this old riddle:

> *The antelope leaped from the bear*
> *and was caught by the lion.*
> *The goose in winter flew south*
> *to be caught by the crocodile.*
> *Awakened by the jackal*
> *the angry lion fell into a pit.*
> *The crocodile's skin has many uses.*

Gaspar then took up a sword and slapped a hanging shield. Melchior, who was sitting in contemplation, was so startled he jumped up from his sitting position, tripped over a camel saddle and fell to the ground.

Balthazar began to laugh, his anger vanished and the riddle made sense to him. "Let them have the camels. We have plenty to carry our provisions. Our scouts must be more vigilant. Obviously we are in a country that is more rowdy than which we have previously passed." At this point Balthazar gained some new respect for Gaspar. In fact, he realized that the power was his own; however, these two other kings may be invaluable to his successful use of power.

For ten days the caravan traveled and water was scarce; even the kings began to ration their own water. On the tenth day a sickness struck the camp: fever, vomiting and diarrhea had dehydrated many, and fifteen died. The caravan sat in the middle of the desert unable to move— over one-third of the camp was ill. King Balthazar himself became gravely ill. He allowed only Gaspar and Melchior to minister to him. A strange friendship was developing among these three. This new relationship began when Balthazar allowed more consultation from Melchior and Gaspar. Melchior realized that he enjoyed not making decisions or giving the orders. He had more time for contemplation and sharing its fruits with Balthazar and Gaspar. Gaspar in turn responded to the respect that Melchior gave him as well as Balthazar's changing attitudes.

Balthazar considered Abdah as a "lucky charm" and ordered him to find water. For five days the caravan sat and buried its dead as ten more died.

Now Abdah had a choice. Since loyalty was not a trait of his people, he could simply leave the kings forever and let them all die. Perhaps he would even come back at some later date to retrieve the booty. However, Abdah had taken a liking to being a well-treated interpreter rather than a camel boy. If the source to which they traveled is as important as they think it is, he might himself some day become a king. Therefore Abdah decided he would find water as quickly as possible and bring several loaded camels back to the kings.

The land across the river was new to Abdah and it was difficult even for this experienced young man to find water. He needed two days to find the water and less than one-half day to return to the caravan.

Balthazar praised Abdah and promised him continued reward. Since the oasis was not far he ordered the caravan to move there. They would remain there until everyone was well.

This was a beautiful oasis with good clear water, trees, grasses and even orchards. Everyone felt a bit uncomfortable because it was not guarded. A place like this in the middle of the desert is too valuable to be left unclaimed. Balthazar sent triple the usual number of scouts and doubled the guard.

Within a few days everyone was returning to good health. Balthazar felt much better and yet not fully recovered. On the third day an army of over two hundred struck them. This time however, the scouts had seen them coming from far off and a defense was prepared as well as a surprise counter-attack. Balthazar's men fought well and easily repulsed the invaders.

Abdah was ordered to interrogate the few prisoners that had been wounded and held captive. He discovered that these were soldiers of King Herod. It was King Herod's plan that the oasis be left unguarded until a caravan settled down comfortably and then attack to obtain booty from the travelers. Over the past few years Herod had been richly rewarded by this strategy.

The very next day a personal emissary from King Herod came to Balthazar's camp with a promise of safe passage if the three kings would visit Herod. Even though it seemed to be a trap, Balthazar felt they had no choice if they wished to cross this land safely.

King Herod's personality was similar to Balthazar's except that he was not just severe, he was cruel. He was not just amused by buffoonery, he was amused by savagery. He not only thought he was a great king, he was ruthless in his kingly actions. Every kingdom had its peasants, servants and slaves. Herod's treatment of these poor people was more savage than most. Even though King Balthazar did nothing to help the poor of his kingdom, he did nothing to make their plight worse as did Herod.

Here is the reason Herod stopped the battle: His astrologers were seeing signs in the sky that indicated a great event was to happen in his kingdom. At this same time the Hebrews were predicting the birth of a great king who would lead them in victory over their enemies (one of which was Herod). Also at this same time Herod began to have nightmares. He saw his own head on a pike, his body pieces strewn on the ground. He saw a king come out of the sun, burning everything in his path including Herod and his family. He saw a worm crawl out of his own skull and turn into a butterfly. Because of these dreams he felt he must question all strangers in order to find this God-king while he is yet an infant and destroy him. Even though he was frightened by the dreams, he felt they might be a good omen warning him in time so that he may destroy the king and like the butterfly, be greater than ever.

The three kings and their army were led to an encampment outside of the city. They knew they were trapped. Herod had over four hundred horsemen and a thousand infantry. They had seen Herod's people and knew this king to be far more savage than themselves. The three kings felt sick to look upon Herod's people. Even Gaspar quit speaking in riddles and jokes and began to speak directly about the situation. Melchior became more silent than usual. Balthazar could only agree with Gaspar.

After meeting with Herod several times over a period of four days, two things became apparent to the kings; Herod had decided that they could be useful to him in finding the newborn king. Balthazar, Gaspar and Melchior had decided that even though they did not like Herod, they must agree to his terms in order to proceed on their journey. An agreement was struck. The kings would be allowed to continue their journey to find "the source" (a concept Herod thought was stupid) under these conditions:

One: The kings leave with only ten soldiers and ten servants. The rest would remain behind until their return. Two: If on their journey they discover the newborn king, they are to send a message to Herod immediately. Three: Failure to return or send a message concerning the king would result in the beheading of every soldier, servant and herder of their caravan. Furthermore they would be hunted down themselves and crucified.

Balthazar, Gaspar and Melchior had now indeed become close friends. Balthazar had been gentled by his lingering sickness. Yet, he remained the natural leader. Gaspar continued to lighten up the arduous travel and yet was not quite the buffoon he used to be. Melchior had become more and more contemplative and continued to navigate

the small group by the stars. Now they traveled only at
night and knew they were coming close to the source.

One night while resting their animals and themselves atop
a high rise, Melchior revealed to Balthazar and Gaspar his
new insight concerning the source of life. The new king
spoken of by Herod may be what they were looking for—
not the head of a turtle, but a man. This new king may
have the power and wisdom to give them a long life and
happiness, protecting them from their enemies and
healing their wounds. Melchior indicated that perhaps the
power of the new king drew them from afar to experience
the power of friendship. Melchior revealed that there were
several small towns in the vicinity and that the stars
indicated that it was somewhere in this area that the
event was to take place.

Balthazar decided that they would camp on that very
spot. His men would depart by twos and search the area
for a newborn king even as unlikely as it was that one
would be born in such humble circumstances. He even
wondered to himself that perhaps his friend Melchior's
mind had been weakened by the arduous journey and was
mistaken concerning what was to take place and where.

Two days later the searchers began returning to camp
and reporting that no birth of males of any status had
taken place within forty miles.

The kings were confused, wondering if the whole trip had
been made in vain. The journey had worn them down.
Balthazar remained sickly. A depressed feeling enervated
even Gasper. Their friendship seemed to heighten the
depression.

By midday of the fourth day of camping on that hill, some
shepherds moving sheep to better pasture passed by. In
conversation, the shepherds indicated that they knew of

only one birth in the vicinity. A few weeks earlier a poor traveling couple was forced to stay at a cave in the hills where animals are kept, and gave birth to a boy. Some shepherds were there to help them. In fact, some of the town's people visited there to share food. The event had brought some people together that had never met before and created some new friendships.

Gaspar suggested they visit the cave, as it might lift their spirits and help them decide what to do next. On the next day they sent Abdah to find the cave and question the people there. The shepherds had given good directions, and Abdah was back to camp by nightfall. He told the kings that it was difficult to see the baby. The parents were a bit shy and secretive. Eager to do something, Balthazar said that if the Hebrew prophesies predicted that a baby king was to be born, they'd have a look. Since most Hebrews are poor, perhaps the Hebrew king will begin poor. Gaspar added that if their king were connected to the source of life he would not be poor for long. Then Melchior continued, "Perhaps the real source of life emerges wherever there is new life. This new life is created as Father-Sky penetrates Mother-Earth, male and female are of the one God."

Gaspar suggested that they disguise themselves until they could determine how they would be received. He also suggested that they send scouts out to be sure Herod was not spying on them. They had agreed that they wouldn't want Herod to know what they were doing until they had found the source and made some decisions.

Looking nondescript and leaving their mounts behind, the three kings led by Abdah began the trek to the cave. It was not yet dusk when they started down a boulder-strewn canyon at the end of which was a corral of sheep under an outcropping of rock.

A tall bearded man along with three young shepherds with heavy staves in their hands came out to greet them. It seemed apparent to the kings that this man was going to question them before he let them proceed. Whether the baby was a king or just another mouth to feed, it would be quite natural for the father to guard against intruders.

The kings stopped some two hundred feet from the corral as the tall man advanced to within twenty feet of them, stopped and asked: "Who are you and what do you want here?" It had been agreed upon beforehand that Melchior would speak for the kings. Melchior answered, "We are wanderers who seek refuge in a cave." The bearded man replied, "Are there no other caves?" Melchior answered, "Yes, however night draws near and we fear we will be lost."

The bearded man continued his inquiry, "Is that your only reason?"

Melchior decided to be more aggressive. "Are you afraid of us or do you
have something to hide?"

"Neither," replied the stranger.

Melchior pushed on, "Then allow us space under the outcropping if not in the cave itself."

The man replied, "This you may do; however do not enter the cave."

Melchior responded, "Do you own the cave? Did you move the rocks that formed its shelter, or were the rocks moved by a greater hand than yours?"

The tall man put down his stave and replied, "Strangers, you are welcome. Sleep under the cropping. Within the cave my wife nurses a newborn babe and I wish to protect them from anyone who might do them harm. I will defend them with my life if need be. The shepherds who herd their sheep hereabouts have promised to help me."

Melchior turned to his companions and said: "Why would shepherds defend strangers with their lives? There must be something special about this baby. Let us do as we are told and perhaps as we gain this man's trust, he will reveal the secret of the child. Perhaps if he has been born to be king through some power we have been called here by that same power to help in some way."

Thus, the three camped there and pretended to be not so curious about the child. The tall man spent time with them in order to know them better. His name was Joseph. On the second day, Joseph's wife Mary brought the child out into the daylight. The kings did not move. They simply reflected on the tenderness of love between mother and child. The also noticed that Joseph, although powerfully built, was tender and almost servant-like towards mother and child. This was indeed a new role for men.

On the third day Mary brought the child over to the kings, who were very much at peace and receiving some much-needed rest. That afternoon Mary allowed each of the kings as well as Abdah to take turns holding the baby. In their own countries men did not hold their babies; in fact they had little to do with infants until they were five or six years of age. Now for the first time each of the kings held and played with a baby. They became so intrigued by the simplicity, strength and warmth that they decided to stay a few more days. Melchior said that the power to grow and be nourished by life was present there. Each man felt awakened as out of sleep. They were open to life, to hope, as never before. Discovering, seeing anew, and loving pebbles as well as mountains, dewdrops as well as oceans, *all people as well as their own families, their hurting selves as well as their happy selves.*

On the fifth day the kings revealed who they were and brought up the remaining men who had been camped on the hill. A party was held in honor of the baby. They laughed, danced and wasted water by dousing everyone present. Gaspar said they needed to wash off their old skin. Shepherds had been invited. The canyon walls echoed with the joy of light-hearted, fulfilled people.

After the party, Melchior could not sleep. He climbed to the top of the canyon wall to meditate. Something was bothering him. He looked to the stars, which were there for everyone to see. He remembered why they had come so far and knew that what he had learned was important. The stars were not just for him; the stars were for everyone. The stars of the heavens were only a reflection of what was already in him, in everyone.

Suddenly Melchior knew what had been bothering him. Herod did not love, but enslaved. Herod had said he wished to honor the new king and yet he dishonored himself. Herod only understood what was before his own eyes and they were greedy eyes. He saw the surface without understanding what brought harmony to the surface and what brought it life. Herod intended to kill this baby and perhaps all babies so that no one could threaten his own life. In the morning, Melchior decided, he will tell the others of his thoughts and let them decide what must be done.

Dawn came suddenly as the sun's rays pierced the fog and splashed against the red canyon walls opposite the cave with a glaring light. Sleeping people, kings, shepherds and animals began to stir. Abdah found Melchior atop the canyon wall wedged between two concealing rocks.

Awakened, Melchior came down and immediately asked to meet with the kings, along with Abdah, Mary and Joseph in the cave. Everyone felt the grave tones and knew Melchior did not speak hastily; he must have spent the better part of the night in contemplation.

After everyone heard Melchior's thoughts, Balthazar commanded that Joseph, Mary and their child come away with him to his kingdom. Gaspar felt this was impossible. They could be found and all killed since their army was held hostage by Herod.

Joseph spoke slowly and hesitantly with Abdah continuing his duties as interpreter. "Friends, we thank you. However we cannot go with you. We cannot go home either. We will travel by a quick and secret path that these shepherds know to Egypt and lose ourselves in a small village until there is a new ruler in the country and we are forgotten. Then we will safely return home to Nazareth." Joseph spoke with such authority that the kings were at a loss to speak.

After a long silence Melchior told Joseph that the stars had signified a great event was to take place somewhere in this area and that was the reason for their journey. He asked Joseph if his child had anything to do with this.

Joseph answered that he had no idea of what they were talking about except these facts: A baby was born and every birth is a great event. The stars did indeed seem to have a strong effect on this place. Shepherds had noticed this. The few townspeople and shepherds who came to the cave seemed to be moved by the place and a spirit of family came over everyone. The Hebrew scripture indicated that a great leader, a savior, was to come from the bloodline of King David of which Joseph himself was a member. Other signs connected with Hebrew scripture and the birth of the king had taken place so that many

Hebrew women at this time hoped to give birth to a king. Mary's conception came under strange circumstances.

The kings sat astounded. A deep silence fell over the cave. Gaspar was the first to speak.

"Joseph is right, we must let them go their own way. We must find a way to trick Herod and leave his kingdom as well as save our men who are held captive by him."

Melchior's thoughts were far from Gaspar's words; these thoughts he would reveal to others later. Melchior now knew that the journey had been necessary so that they might be able to understand the event. A new light, a new guide to understanding had entered the world. The one God had penetrated man's world and brought forth his spirit in mankind.

Each king had some gold, incense and myrrh for trading as well as ceremonial purposes. They agreed to give these gifts to Joseph. If bribes were needed as well as necessities to be bought in Egypt, these gifts would help.

Balthazar had already developed a plan of action and would not allow anyone to change his mind. He knew he was dying. Under his thick robes, he had lost much weight and his lungs ached. He would go back to Herod and keep him occupied with stories as if awaiting the arrival of the other kings. Meanwhile, he would prepare his men for a mass escape. If he were lucky he could save two-thirds of his men. While he was occupying Herod with stories, and then the mass escape, Mary, Joseph and the two kings would leave with the shepherds for Egypt. Once in Egypt, Mary and Joseph could continue on to find a home. Gaspar and Melchior could travel up the great river to the point where they had first met and race home to their respective kingdoms. Balthazar himself did not expect to return. He would give Gaspar the signs and symbols of authority over his kingdom. Abdah insisted upon remaining with Balthazar and continuing as his interpreter.

No one objected to Balthazar's plan even though they knew he and Abdah were sacrificing themselves. Everyone there understood now that life erupts on this earth and then returns to its source. As the mother and father love their child, so do the Earth Mother and Father, the right and left hands of the all-embracing God. Everyone was at peace. Each one would have their own role in life and in death.

With great wisdom and yet with tearful compassion the friends separated. Mary, Joseph and child fled safely into Egypt. Gaspar and Melchior returned without incident to their kingdoms. Balthazar was never heard from again. The few of his army that had escaped Herod and returned home had last known Balthazar and Abdah to be indulging Herod in colorful stories.

Melchior had returned home as a beggar. No one knew who he was. He melted in with the crowds and yet became known as a "seer," a seer with a new God, a new religion, a new way of living. His preaching began in small villages, far from the center of the kingdom. He told no one who he was. However, as he developed a small following and moved closer to the city, his own son, the present ruler, imprisoned him.

Melchior's wife and son were severe rulers, while Melchior did not wish to be treated any differently than the poorest of the kingdom. He persisted in not declaring who he was. One day, a survivor among the men who had traveled with Melchior returned to the kingdom and told Melchior's son of his father's adventures. Melchior's son promoted this man to lieutenant in charge of the king's prisoners. It was in this position that he recognized Melchior.

The wife and son could not believe that it was Melchior because he had changed physically and mentally. His thinking and preaching undermined the power of the kings. They decided that all should be kept secret. The lieutenant was warned that he would die if any of this leaked out to the people. Melchior would be restricted to a garden compound for the rest of his days. Knowing nothing of any of this at the time, I was taken off the streets and ordered into his service.

For ten years Melchior spoke to no one but me. Melchior died peacefully and had no intentions of putting this story in writing. However, as he has been dead some eight years and I waste away, I know the world needs to know this story and be aware of the great event as foretold in legend and in the stars.

Everyone in this kingdom calls the garden where Melchior spent his last years, "The garden of the dark hut." Straining to see through the very thin cracks in the thick wall that surrounds the garden, the people could see only the windowless hut in the middle. One of my duties was to keep any larger holes filled. I, who was allowed to enter and spend time with Melchior, see the garden as a holy place, full of delights. Melchior taught me this.

Any place one chooses can become a place of balance and beauty if man is wise enough to understand the necessary harmony between the inner and outer sphere. Melchior cherished all living and nonliving in the garden. He polished small stones with his hands. He patiently watched seeds sprout through cracks in the rocks and bloom in full sun. He praised the small field mouse as it came from its mother's womb and grew to maturity. He seemed to pierce the clear blue sky with his intent stare. He loved the clouds, studied the stars and danced in the rain. He opened his arms to both the sun and moon and thanked them for being there. He felt connected to human *life. He would thoughtfully stamp the earth with his feet and then laughingly say that people in Gaspar's kingdom felt the vibration. He looked intently at the sky and said he could see many kingdoms and the people there could see him if they know how. He closed his eyes sitting in contemplation and he would say afterwards that he had joined with others who were very far away. Sometimes, he joined with Balthazar and sometimes he joined with the one God. He said that if men learned to love one another as well as the earth and its creatures, then the inner and outer sphere would be in harmony and the surface of the earth would be a garden of delights.*

Finally, whenever I queried Melchior about the child he found in Bethlehem, he had little to say. Routinely, I would ask him if he had further revelations concerning the child and he would query me of any news from the outside concerning a new king. There never was. Melchior had only this to say: "The one God had entered the world in a special way through that baby," and Melchior's greatest joy was to have held him. He believed that the baby lived somewhere and was growing into manhood.

Thus, I end Melchior's story with my own understanding of kingship, which each man inherits at birth. Each one of us is a king.

John awoke and realized the arcade was almost deserted. It was only two in the afternoon. He thought it would be best that he close up for the day. He cleaned up the place and locked it. He headed out onto the street and realized it had been snowing all day, and traffic was moving slowly. It looked like everyone would be snowed in for Christmas. People on the street were hurrying every which way hoping to get home before gridlock set in. With gridlock downtown nothing moved for long stretches of time and people would be arriving home on

Christmas Eve hours later than they had planned. John was not in a hurry. He had no particular reason to be home quickly; however, whenever stories came to his mind like the two this day he liked to write them down as soon as possible, before the details were forgotten.

John was always mystified by the diversity of people he saw on the streets and was overwhelmed by the fact that the people he actually saw were such an infinitesimal number compared to all the people on earth or all the people that had ever been or will be on earth. He would be happy to get home to the warmth of his apartment, sip the liqueur given to him as a gift and contemplate the mystery of people and write his stories.

John was surprised how little time he had to wait for the bus. He realized however that the ride home would be very slow going. At the very next stop a couple of teenagers entered the bus. The girl was heavily pregnant and had to be helped by the boy. She looked like she should be giving birth at any time now. John's thought went back to the manger scene. The Jesus, Mary and Joseph there were like Hollywood cutouts; they were not real looking. The couple who were now trying to find enough change to pay the bus fare was for real. Without saying a word, John got up from his seat and paid the fare for them. He sat back down and another story filled his imagination:

Miracle Grandpa

"Joe, I don't want to wait any longer. I want to get married now."

"No, I won't get married till I have a steady job. Construction around here is down. Everyone is saying it will be down for a long time. Look Mary, they're building a big factory in Bardstown, Kentucky; I hear they need

carpenters. It's a two-year job minimum and may be permanent. The job doesn't start for six, seven, maybe eight months but they're hiring now. I'll drive down tomorrow and apply. If I get the job, I'll be back on Friday. We'll plan to get married and...."

"And if you don't get the job?"

"Then we'll wait—I don't want a wife and someday a child that I can't support."

"But I have a job."

"It just doesn't make enough money."

"It would be cheaper for the two of us to live together."

"No, it won't work. If you get pregnant, then we're in big money trouble."

"Sometimes, Joe, I wished we lived in a different place, a different time, where making money didn't control everything we do."

"I love you, honey. Let's pray that I get the job—then everything will be all right—I'll see you Friday—wish me luck."

"Take care, Joe. I love you."

Mary went to bed that night in her small two-room apartment on the near- west side of Cleveland. She was troubled. Yet, she was in love with a good, sensitive man—no drugs, no temper, and a responsible yet easy attitude was about him—that made all the difference.

Mary thought about the job Joe would be seeking the next day and prayed to her own unknown God that Joe be safe *and if it were God's will the job would be his—would be theirs.*

Suddenly, Mary became feverish, dizzy almost to the point of nausea. She blanked out. She was aware of her body traveling through time and space, leaving earth far behind. Planets and galaxies rushed by. All emanated from a spiraling cone, a tunnel, which she was falling through at ever-increasing speed. Coming from the end of the tunnel was a life force the size of a small seed. Clearly it was coming at her and meant to penetrate her—to knife into her body and explode there. At the moment it hit her, it disappeared and an aura of warm light surrounded her. A question was asked: "Will you protect Him? Will you protect Him?" The suffering of the world was manifested to her. The starving, the maimed, the mentally ill, distorted bodies and distorted minds of hundreds of thousands of people pressed down on her. Filled with compassion for all of humanity, Mary entered the light with a firm resolve and a silent "Yes."

Mary awoke the next morning calm and at peace even though the meaning of the dream was unclear to her. She thought of Joe and prayed again that he would be safe and the job theirs. Since she worked the evening shift as a nurse's aide, she had the day to herself. She felt a little nausea and decided she was getting the flu and went back to bed after breakfast. It was a restless sleep and the phrase "Will you protect Him?" repeated over and over in her mind. She dreamed she was pregnant and about to have a baby. She awoke with a startle. She knew she had to protect a baby. What baby?

Joe came home on Thursday elated that he had a guaranteed job even though it wouldn't be for another nine months. He and Mary could plan to get married in seven or eight months, go to Bardstown, find a place to live and enjoy their new life together.

"If we are very careful with our money now—no engagement ring, no honeymoon, no luxuries until we are secure as husband and wife in our new home, we'll have enough until I begin work in Bardstown."

Mary and Joe were in ecstasy and had never been happier together. However, Mary decided she must confront the recurring dreams and the morning sickness, which she had kept secret from Joe. She made an appointment with the old family doctor whom she had gone to since childhood and who could keep a secret. The kindly old man was gentle in telling Mary that he had no idea why she had those dreams but that she was indeed about two months pregnant. Knowing she wasn't married, he did not know what her reaction would be. Oddly enough, the news of pregnancy did not panic her. For some reason the warmth and peace she felt in that dream remained with her. For some reason the phenomenon was natural to her. Yet, Joe was another problem. Her clothes didn't fit her and soon it would be obvious to everyone. How could she possibly convince him of her virginity? How could he possibly believe her? Why does she believe this?

"A whore, is that what you are? How could you pretend with me? You couldn't possibly love the guy. I know you love me. What were you looking for—experiences? Why didn't you seduce me? I'm the guy you're supposed to marry. What about disease? I don't want to know who it was. Are you sure he loves you? Are you sure he doesn't make it with every chick he meets? Are you sure he doesn't have AIDS, that you won't have AIDS, that the baby won't have AIDS? Damn, how could you...?"

Joe slammed the door shut and left. Mary cried and cried. A week went by and she hadn't heard from Joe. She needed someone to talk to. Her Aunt Liz might help. Liz counseled unwed mothers and was pregnant herself with her third child. Mary would be the first unwed mother in her family—perhaps Liz could soften the blow to her parents, brothers, and sisters.

Mary called in sick to work and went to visit Liz that evening. Her uncle had gone bowling and the kids were in bed. They had a couple of hours of quiet conversation over coffee, cheese and crackers at the kitchen table. Liz fumbled her cheese-covered cracker when Mary told her the news. Liz would have been more surprised if she had not known how much in love Joe and Mary were. However, when she asked how Joe felt about it and Mary said he wasn't the father; Liz gasped a deep breath and almost choked on her cracker. Liz thought Mary must be withholding information as many of her unwed mothers do, except that she knew her niece to be straightforward and honest and had always confided in her. The dream that Mary told was unbelievable. Liz thought something very traumatic must have happened to her niece and that counseling beyond her capabilities was in order. Yet, Mary had no other symptoms. She was calm and together. Liz also remembered that she herself had a dream some months past. In Liz's dream Mary gave birth to a healthy boy and Liz was excitedly telling the family. In the dream Liz had accepted the whole situation with joy and without question. Liz decided she would not press Mary.

"Are you sure?"

"Yes!"

"How do you feel about this and what does Joe think?

"I haven't seen him since I told him."

"What will you do now?"

"Have a baby and help it grow into a healthy adult."

"Are you ready for that?"

"Yes!"

"What can I do to help?"

"Be there with me when I tell the family; soften the blow and don't let them ask too many questions. Please don't let Bill harangue me about this being a bastard and should be aborted. It wouldn't hurt me but it would cause all kinds of argument in the family."

"Perhaps we ought to tell Bill first and beg him to stay out of it. We'll go together on Thursday night to Bill's place and see the rest of the family on Saturday."

The next morning Mary slept in and was fixing coffee about 11 A.M. when someone knocked on the door. It was Joe with a half-dozen doughnuts, a bouquet of flowers and cheap engagement ring.

"Look, Mary, if you're going to have a baby it will be mine no matter where it came from," were Joe's first words. Mary was so shocked she nearly fainted. She lost her breath in Joe's loving embrace.

"Joe, why are you doing this?"

"Look Mary, I loved you before and I realized that I love you now. Liz called me last night after you left her place and told me about your conversation, your dream, her dream, all of it. She wanted to know where I really stood in your life. I didn't know. After her call I fell asleep and had a dream of my own. A voice kept saying 'Protect Mary and her baby; love them no matter what happens.' That voice calmed me and let me know where my heart really

was. I no longer have questions. I only wish to look to our future."

Six months later Mary, more ripely pregnant than expected and sticking out as big as a house, calmly boarded the old 1976 Chevy that Joe had fought to keep running. Having said good-bye to their friends and family the night before, Mary and Joe set out for Bardstown, Kentucky and Joe's new job, their new home and new life together. The weather did not cooperate from the start— drizzle turned into snow. They were heading south on the freeway and into one of the biggest snowstorms of the decade. They hadn't gotten much past Mansfield when state troopers ordered them off the freeway onto traffic- clogged secondary roads. Cars were stranded all over. Joe, being a skillful driver kept moving, using untrafficked roads to avoid the jam-ups. Mary read the map and was a good navigator in this respect.

They should have been in Bardstown by now and here they were still picking their way through backcountry roads in southern Ohio. It was nearly dusk; the car was burning oil and nearly out of gas and Mary was having frequent contractions. When Joe was unsure of where he was, he pulled up to an old barn just off the road; they just couldn't go on. There was well over a foot of snow and it was still coming down hard. He could hardly see the road and was lucky to see the barn when a gust of wind cleared his view for a moment.

"Where is the farmhouse? It must be here someplace. I can't see a thing."

"Joe, I think the baby is going to come soon."

Joe rushed to the barn and pushed the huge door back. It was stocked with bales of hay and there were a few animals in their stalls. Joe thought it would be warmer in the barn rather than in an out-of-gas automobile. Outside he just couldn't see well enough to tell in what direction the farmhouse might be. He helped Mary out of the car and into the barn. There were several cows, a calf, a young horse, a cat and her kittens to share the night. Snug in the hay, that night Joe and Mary delivered a healthy boy child. Mary kept her baby close to her body underneath her clothes and Joe held them both as they fell asleep.

Joe awoke with a start. A dog barked and sniffed at the barn door. Everything else was silent and still. Then came the crunch of boots and the barn door squeaked open, allowing the glare of daylight to pour into the dark barn. A man and a boy stood at the doorway.

"Saw your car in front of my barn; I came to see if you're all right."

"Yes. Thank you."

"How many of you are there?"

"Myself, my wife and baby."

"Well come on in, get up and come to my house for some coffee and breakfast, Can your car run?"

"We're nearly out of gas."

"I can help you there. That was some storm; telephone lines are down, roads are impassable. There is nearly three feet of snow. You must stay till tomorrow. The highway patrol wants everyone to stay off the roads."

"This is my boy Pete and I'm Jake Cutter. What's your name?"

"I'm Joe; this is Mary and our baby."

"What's the baby's name?"

"I don't know, he was born in your barn last night."

"You don't say, you can't beat that; born in my barn. Wait till Ruthie hears this. Is he okay?"

"He seems to be."

"Well come on, let's get in the house and have Ruthie check him over."

Joe and Mary spent that day and night with the Cutters. Neighbors hitched a team of horses to a sleigh and came over to visit. Everyone sat around the wood-burning stove, laughed, sang and told stories. No story could beat Jake's—the one about the baby born in his barn. Since that baby was some weeks early Mary and Joe hadn't made a decision about what to name him. Some of the day was passed by everyone trying to name the baby and giving reasons why their name was a good one. Jake finally spoke up.

"My name really isn't Jake; it's Joshua. All of my life I have liked the name Joshua, but was so accustomed to everyone calling me Jake that I haven't used my real name. When I was a small boy my friends made fun of the name Joshua. They would yell out "Osh Gosh by Gosh, Oshua Goshua by Joshua." So I never used the name. You might say this is a prideful suggestion but I would be mighty proud if you call that son of yours Joshua."

Both Joe and Mary knew instantly that that was the name for their son.

Well, Joshua didn't grow up in Bardstown; in fact hard times came there too and the factory was never finished.

He ended up in Pittsburgh through his grade school years and then back to Cleveland as a teenager. The rest of his life is well known to most people. Joshua became a wanderer and until about the age of thirty seemed to have a quiet influence on some important people. Some say he even saw the Pope on several occasions.

When Joshua was about thirty, people began to create a myth about him and a movement sprang up from some of his ideas: The "One God, One Universe, One World" movement. Its symbol was three rings intertwined with a triangle. I'm not sure if Joshua approved of the movement, some of the people in it, or its tactics. Yet he would speak at public gatherings all over the world. He spoke in many languages and inspired many people. That's when he made enemies and that's why on that beautiful spring day he was shot to death while speaking to a crowd outside the Nations building in New York City.

There was a great stir after Joshua's death because no one could locate his body. Some say he never died, that he is in prison or hiding someplace. His close friends say that he did die and that his spirit had appeared to them. Whatever the case, his death caused a great uproar all over the world and many of his followers have been jailed throughout the world as rabble-rousers, traitors, spies, and unpatriotic citizens of their respective countries.

A couple of years ago, when I thought I was close to death, I dictated my story of Joe and Mary to my friend Shirley. Somebody got a hold of it recently and published it. Now I have all those reporters wanting to talk to me, wanting more details of Joshua's early life. The doctors won't let them in and I don't want to see them anyway. I prefer to say what I have to say to Shirley.

For the record this is Jake Cutter talking, alive and kicking when I should be—and most people thought I would be—

dead. The people around this hospital call me the "miracle grandpa." Now, mind you, I don't have any grandchildren. Technically, I'm not a grandpa. At 96, I'm old enough to be called one. Anyway, about two weeks ago I died and the doctors brought me back to life. I went through one of those "life after life" experiences that happen to people who have died and been brought back by modern medicine.

Here's what happened: In my sleep I left my body and was floating near the door just as Shirley entered the room. I saw her run out and call a nurse, who came in and began mouth-to-mouth resuscitation on my old broken-down body. I was wondering why she was doing it, because the body was worn out. Doctors came in with equipment and began to try to bring me back. Suddenly I began to walk down the hallway. There was an open door at the end and it was like walking out of the barn into the fields on a beautiful spring day. Standing there were the people I loved—Ruthie, Peter, Mary, Joe and Joshua. Even though we were just standing there, it felt like we were hugging one another. Everyone was happy. It felt like the day we sat around the wood burner trying to name the new baby, Joshua. Then I began to ache—the same ache I had when each of them had died. I knew I couldn't stay with them. For some reason I had to live longer. I turned from them with determination and walked back into the barn. I awoke with Shirley and the doctors standing over me. The doctor said, "You're a miracle, Grandpa!"

While lying here over the past week I have been wondering what purpose there is for a sickly old man in this world. Why couldn't I have stayed with my friends? Part of the answer came to me this morning when Shirley told me about all the news people. I decided I had better dictate more of what I know about Joshua's early life.

As I said before, after Joshua was born in my barn, Joe and Mary became friends of mine. I helped them get to Bardstown and find a place to rent. They were dirt poor and it wasn't easy for them especially with Joe being black and Mary white. People don't like that mixing. Joshua himself was somewhere in between. When he was old enough to have friends and enemies, his friends saw him as white or black depending on their own color; his enemies saw him the opposite of themselves. I simply saw him as Joshua and it never entered my mind whether he looked more white or black. Of course as an infant, none of this mattered to him since he was loved and cared for by Joe and Mary. The fact was that Mary and Joe had very few friends because of racial prejudice and yet they were a couple of the friendliest young people I had ever met. I saw Joshua about every six months, as an infant, toddler and child, when Joe and Mary came to visit. He developed rather normally, yet he was a charmer, a characteristic that stayed with him his whole life. Anyway, Joe and Mary barely eked out a living in Bardstown. Work had hardly begun on the factory when they stopped building because of the sluggish economy. Competition for work there was cutthroat and Joe wasn't the cutthroat type. My brother in Pittsburgh found construction work for him and they moved into a slummy area there. I didn't see Joshua much for the next eight years. Joe and Mary wrote me but it was the usual day-to-day family life—nothing that stands out in my mind.

When Joshua was about twelve or thirteen Joe and Mary moved back to Cleveland. The economy had picked up and a whole lot of construction was being done there. They bought a HUD home in the Tremont area on the near-west side. It was a mixed neighborhood of white, black, Hispanic, and Asian, so they felt comfortable there. During these years they visited Ruthie, Peter and me every summer. Peter and Joshua would spend long hours walking the fields, fishing and whatever else young boys do. They were great friends even though Peter was six years older than Joshua. I didn't give Joshua chores. He helped Peter with his chores, which gave them more free time to play together. That was okay by me. Of course, sometimes the work at hand demands little time for play, like when we're harvesting hay or wheat; then we all work from sunup to sundown. Throughout his whole life Joshua would come back to the farm, to help with chores and walk the woods and fields. Sometimes he would camp by himself in the woods for a week at a time.

Back to Cleveland! Joshua went to Lincoln Intermediate School and then to West Tech High School. Although everyone knew he was bright and talented, his grade average was only a high "B." Some teachers didn't like him because when there was injustice he never backed down. He took his lickings for that. His homework wasn't always done either, because he was always ready to put it aside in order to help someone in trouble. Coaches of every sport were after him to play their sport because it was evident that he had a lot of physical gifts. In gym class he was a standout. However, he shied away form the competitive sports except for cross-country, which he ran for two years. He quit that his senior year even though he was one of the top ten in the state the year before. He said he liked running but not the competition. The coach hated him for that. He also played the trumpet some and took small parts in school plays. Everyone said he had talent, which he did not seem to care to develop. Joe and Mary were awfully patient with him.

The one characteristic that always remained was Joshua's friendliness to everyone and his willingness to help out. As I indicated before, some saw him white and some saw him black, so he had enemies. A couple of times he was jumped and beaten up. The girls liked him. Most were upset because he simply wanted to be their friend. Some of the girls started a rumor out of jealousy that he was gay.

However there was no evidence of this on the boy's side and the rumor faded out quickly. He tended to treat everyone with friendliness—no matter what their social status, their race, their gang or sexual orientation.

Joe died in a construction accident when Joshua was a senior in high school. Some say that this was so traumatic for Joshua that it was the reason he didn't go to college. I can tell you for a fact that isn't true. Joshua never had the intention of going to college. In fact, he and my boy Peter always planned to travel around the world once Joshua graduated from high school. Peter worked at a large corporate firm down the road and was saving money for that purpose. When Joshua graduated, he and Peter traveled together from time to time to places all over the world. Those two boys sent post cards from all over. They had crisscrossed the Mother-Earth at least three times in ten years. From time to time they traveled separately and even settled for a short while in different places. Mary might get a card from Joshua from Maine. I might get one from Peter in India. Then again, we both might get postcards from Ethiopia or the Sudan. They picked up a smattering of many different languages—a talent that was genius in Joshua and a mild surprise to me in Peter.

After a while, Mary came to live with us on the farm and Joshua, Peter and their buddies would come every once in a while to spend some time. They would sit around and laugh and talk, take long walks and sometimes camp in the woods. They also did all my chores. Harvest was a snap when they were around. There was no doubt about it; Peter and the others looked up to Joshua. He had a lot of wisdom and I began to believe Mary concerning the strange circumstances of his birth—that she was not a genetic freak—that a mysterious force had brought Joshua to this world. At the time, I thought of Joshua in terms of him being a kindly alien. Yet as I grew older I began to understand more of what he said and believed

*that he did come from the world of "life after life." I didn't
tell anyone this at that time.*

*Mary and Joe did not attend any particular church and
neither did Joshua. He attended religious ceremonies
wherever and whenever it pleased him. When he spoke he
often based his reasoning on a loving creator God whose
life and breath permeates each of us. The paradox of evil
being mixed up with a loving God was not uncomfortable
to him. He simply mentioned that God loves and resides in
each of us and we must avoid doing evil to one another
and on the other hand go out of our way to help one
another.*

*Joshua, Peter and their closest friends were not really a
part of the "One God, One Universe, One World Movement"
even though Joshua's ideas had sparked it. For many,
Joshua's teachings became a political theory to change
governments. For Joshua his teachings were a conversion
for one person at a time.*

*Mary was sitting with me in the kitchen when Joshua was
killed. We were watching the news when they showed the
shooting on the steps of the U.N. where he was speaking.
Mary shuddered and simply sat there resolutely. I thought
I heard her say, "Thy will be done." I ached inside just as I
did when Ruthie died. Yet when Mary spoke, a peaceful
surrender came over me and the ache stopped. A year
later my son, Peter, was killed in a New York slum while
carrying some necessities to some poor folk. When Joshua
was killed I knew Peter would be also. Such good men
living out a dream for mankind were wasted by evil forces
that reached out to corrupt men.*

*Not long after Peter died, Mary died. She made coffee in
the morning as was her custom and then took the pickup
truck to look in on a neighbor gal who was about to have
a baby and had been abandoned by her husband. While*

she was visiting a storm came up. She left the gal's house in the middle of the storm because she knew I wasn't feeling well. She never arrived home. Her body was never found. The pickup was out of gas alongside the road in a snowdrift with the ignition on. I simply waved goodbye to Mary in my prayers and reminded myself that she yet lives, as do all the others. It was at this time that I began to more fully understand Joshua. I began to understand that eating, drinking, talking and working together bound us in spirit as well as flesh.

Come to think of it—now I think I know why I was sent back from death. While I cultivated fields and harvested food for animals and people, Joshua and Peter were cultivating and harvesting souls for God. Both are important works. I simply hadn't done enough for souls. I've been given time for at least one more planting and one more harvest.

Before John realized it, the young couple was leaving the bus. He watched them through the bus window disappear into the whirling snow in the direction of the emergency room entrance to the hospital. John thought, "It may not be a virgin birth and it may not be a boy, but that child is as special as any other. Maybe given the right circumstances that child could add a little peace and love to this earth."

He pulled the line to signal the driver and disembarked at his stop. He quickly crossed the street and began to climb the stairs to his apartment. He wasn't sure if he was climbing to a womb or a tomb. It was, however, the place where he wrote his stories. He wrote them and left them in piles scattered around the place. Some years later John would fall asleep and not awaken in that room. Some young housecleaner would take all of John's trash and burn it. John was certain of this.

Beyond Solitude

The desert floor is dark on a night with no moon. Somewhere on a strip of road passing over that ebony plain, a solitary automobile courses with headlights revealing the sharp shadows of cacti and sagebrush as they strobe at the edge of that fleeting somewhere.

From behind the wheel Paul leaned over, lit the cigarette he had been fingering, stretched his big frame, relaxed and slowly surveyed the bejeweled sky. It was two in the morning and Paul was well on his way from San Francisco to Salt Lake City on government business. The huge canopy of flickering stars gave thought of his own small life in contrast to all life and the work of all men. Within this speeding car, this time capsule cutting a hole in the emptiness, the many roles he played in life melted into one. With clarity he pictured the people he had known throughout his life, from the skinny little boy that he had been to the prematurely grey military officer that he was now.

Paul's thoughts became focused on the great Milky Way spread out above him. Gradually each star became a person, each with its own personal beauty and solitude; and yet in relation to one another, part of a pattern, a design, the oneness of the firmament.

Suddenly a star exploded brightly, fled across the sky and disintegrated into the dark. At that moment Paul felt that he could reflect on, understand and love each person in his or her precious individuality, preventing any one of them from hurling themselves so finally to destruction.

Now, both of Paul's hands were on the wheel, a quick pull left, then back right, his foot to the brake pedal; he slowly applied pressure to bring the car to a smooth halt. He shoved the gearshift into reverse and backed along the road and then onto the soft shoulder ahead of a parked vehicle. As he turned off the engine, he opened the door and slid off the seat to stand alone. He took a deep breath of the cool dry desert air. His senses responded to the peculiar beauty of the night desert; first the silence, then the dry cool dusty smell that he could almost taste, the gritty sound of his shoes against the sand. Finally his eyes could make out the desert forms without the aid of headlights. A small fire shone a short distance off the road as if a very small star tired of hovering high had come down to rest there.

No one was near the campfire, which was crackling and hissing, keeping conversation with itself. Paul thought that the people from the disabled vehicle had already been picked up by a passing motorist, and merely forgot to put out the fire. He scooped a double handful of sand and was about to begin extinguishing the blaze when from the shadows, outside of the range of light, a man's voice came, "Hello, how are you?" as if he had met an old friend on a street corner.

"Just fine," answered Paul, "Can I help you?"

"Yes," the deep male voice from the shadows replied, "but in a different way than you expect. Will you sit by the fire with me and talk for awhile?"

With these words the shadow figure came into the light and Paul saw a very tall, lean, delicate man in suit and tie. Saying nothing more, the man sat opposite him and invited Paul to sit. Curious but suspicious, Paul held fast to the stranger's stare, their senses so intensely finding one another that all else disappeared from their attention. After a short silence the man began to speak.

"Have you ever thought much about the unidentified flying objects many people claim to see? You know, the type of reports that seem to bring to reality all the fanciful projections of men who might someday discover other worlds."

The man gestured to the heavens and initially Paul followed the outstretched arm with his eyes but then quickly drew down, on guard, to watch the stranger whose gentle voice seemed to confuse even more his unexplained presence.

The man continued noticing Paul's growing wariness, "Please don't think of me as a madman. I'm not here to do harm but to ask your help. I only ask that you hear me out before you choose."

Paul said nothing and wondered what he had gotten himself into and just how could he get to his car and away from this place and the man.

"Imagine if you would," the man started, "another planet with human beings very similar to those on earth. Imagine these people superior to you in all technologies. However, imagine them with no particular purpose or end. Through science these people have developed tremendous restorative techniques and are on the verge of prolonging life indefinitely. With no knowledge in an end beyond themselves and with the growing realization of these powers, their craving to hold onto life becomes an obsession. Yet when life itself is the only purpose many see that time is a heavy weight. Many have resorted to suicide because they are simply tired of living, while the majority tenaciously clings to their own lives at all cost. Throughout all this, scientists are feverishly working, trying to perfect extended life, while artists and entertainers of all types are working to provide amusement and diversion suitable to extended life...for some a great boredom, for others, a great frustration. Actually, this describes the planet from which I came."

Paul stood and began to excuse himself from the stranger. Paul felt clear headed and very much in control. He saw no weapons and the man was obviously not as strong or quick as he was. Then he sat down again, deciding it would be interesting to hear this eccentric's full story.

"There is a very small group of us there," the man continued, "that have believed for all time that there is meaning to life, a purpose for which life is spent, a purpose towards which life grows. This purpose is unknowable in a perfect sense. Our lives are regulated by the just law of a God who is the creator of life and of all existence and yet whose mysterious presence is somehow not understood by us. Even our most prophetic voices could not give understanding. Our prophets said someone would be born onto time into the universe who would also be present in the life of God and who would redeem our errors of understanding by a life of example and teaching. Your planet was revealed to us. We came secretly, studied your prophets and discovered Christ, Buddha, and an assortment of holy men and women who exemplified a meaning in life. The diversity by which your people understood their words became alarming. In another revelation, an oracle spoke of you and that we should seek you out and ask you to interpret the messages that these holy men and women brought to Earth. I am asking you to come with me to my planet and to help us."

All the while the stranger spoke, Paul was gradually withdrawing into his own mind. The stranger, the fire, the road, the desert were all unreal; even with 2,000 miles separating them, only his home and family were real and only the sights and sounds of his home and warmth of his family became valid.

"I can't go anyplace with you. I can't say that I believe a word you've said. I'm leaving."

"Paul!" There was a pleading in the man's voice, "Our oracle said that you would say these very words, and she said, 'Tell him, unless he leave mother, father, brother, sister, and family for my sake, he shall not be perfect.'"

"I'm just a simple man, I'm not a scholar. I don't want to be perfect and I don't believe a word you're saying. I'm a military man and am not about to teach anyone anything."

"The words of scripture, whether written in Sanskrit, Hebrew, Aramaic, Mandarin, German or any other language, are nothing compared to the change that takes place in the heart of a human. The words are an inadequate means to understanding. This is why we need you. We need not words; we need a life."

"Look, if what you say is true, why didn't God come to me? Why didn't an angel appear to me, a spirit vision? I hear only you. Your words are the words of a stranger. You are very confused and hallucinating. You're trying to tell me I'm supposed to leave Earth, leave everyone I know, everything I value, and go to some distant planet. Is that car over there your spaceship? I've had enough entertainment for one evening." Paul turned his back on the man and began walking to his car.

The man shouted, "I ask you in all sincerity and love to come with me. We need you! Come! All must be done tonight. The stars await us beyond this desert's solitude."

Giorgio in the Year 2153

My name is Giorgio. I am seventeen years old and live in the year 2153. I live where few people live—within a forest preserve. I live as practically no one else does because I am one of the few "unchosen" to survive. I use the obsolete art of writing because I have no other means to record my thought and no one with whom to talk. I am well aware that perhaps no one will ever read this. I write to organize my thoughts, to help myself study them and arrive at conclusions. My great-grandma would say, "When intuition and written thought are complementary, you will know that you are making the right choice."

My great-grandma, who taught me to write, has most certainly died in prison since it has been over six months since the day they netted her. If I am netted, I will have left behind this writing with the hope that some day someone will read my thought and discover the me-that-had-been. I do believe I have lived an altogether different life than most anyone else on earth. I have some knowledge and ideas that I might contribute to the future.

My mother had become pregnant without "AC," approved choice. In other words, she didn't choose to become pregnant nor did she have approval from the Authority to give birth. My mother was very young, thirteen years of age, when she was raped by a stranger and conceived me. Birthing is well regulated on earth by the Authority and most women conceive through artificial insemination under a strict scientific formula. "Unauthorized" fetuses are immediately aborted. Many receive their children from the labs without the necessity of enduring a pregnancy. However, because my mother was so very young and able to hide the rape from her mother, she herself did not fully realize that she was pregnant until she was near birthing time. When her mother, my grandmother, finally discovered the truth, she was frightened. To give birth to an unauthorized baby is to suffer imprisonment, and the baby is destroyed. There are greater punishments for those who raise unauthorized children. Further complicating the matter, my grandma's mother, my great-grandma, lived in the forest preserve. If my mother had gone to the authorities at that late date in the pregnancy, an investigation would have been conducted and the link to my great-grandma discovered. This would bring further investigation and hardship on my mother and her mother.

Let me explain.... In this society my great-grandma is considered a witch. She lived off the land in the unconditioned air of the forest preserve. It is forbidden to live in the preserve and is believed to be dangerous to a person's health unless you are a witch. The authorities had removed almost everyone from the forest preserve and allowed the few who were not caught to simply die off. More recently the Authority had developed the means to mass-produce oxygen. In the near future, the remaining preserves will be destroyed.

My great-grandma is considered a witch because she survived in the preserve, practiced forbidden ancient craft, and believed in long-ago discarded illusions. My great-grandma practiced agriculture and ate food grown in soil. Everyone else eats the synthetic foods produced by the Authority. The synthetic food is considered the basis of health and longevity in the civilization. My great-grandma knew how to read and write, and she practiced these arts. Everyone else knows that interactive virtual reality is more fulfilling and mind-expanding. The incantations of reading and the symbols of writing are thought to be evil and designed to weaken the bonds that hold the community together. My great-grandma fraternized with animals. Everyone else knows that these diseased, dirty creatures are throwbacks from ancient time, and all human contact with them is to be avoided. In general, my great-grandma was considered a step backwards in the evolutionary scheme of life and her ways are considered witchcraft in the present era as condemned by the Third Scientocratic Authority Counsel (SAC).

Perhaps now you can understand why my mother and grandmother were in a dilemma. If the baby, me, were legally terminated the investigation would begin. If the connection with my great-grandma were discovered, my mother and grandma would be suspect and watched for their entire lives.

Well, one aspect of the decision was made for them. I was born a few weeks ahead of schedule. Now, they couldn't possibly go to the authorities and they didn't have the heart to dismember me and throw me into the disposal as now everyone else does in similar situations. As you can guess, I was secreted away to my great-grandma in the forest where I have lived ever since, never seeing my mother or grandmother as they had all agreed.

Of course, since I grew up with great-grandma, I found her way of life making much sense to me. It was natural and undeserving of the label "witchcraft." I suppose if I attempted to live outside this preserve, I would be labeled and terminated.

Two hundred years ago the scientific revolution began to impact heavily on the earth and the future way of life. Scientific thought became the ultimate authority for all ecological, political, sociological, and psychological decisions. The new world government that evolved in about 2045 A.D. became known as the "Scientocratic Authority Counsel." The SAC made all decisions on behalf of the planet according to strict scientific principles. The SAC regulated all life on earth. The SAC has been able to extend human life so that the average individual may now live to two hundred years of age. Of course birthing, entertainment, work and all else are strictly controlled by the scientific principles. The only place on earth where an individual may escape these controls is in the forest preserves yet still needed to produce oxygen.

At this point in my life I remain happy to be alive. However, my future looks dim. At least my future will not be interminably long. My great-grandma tells me that I should probably not live past one hundred years of age in the forest. I am content with that. On the other hand, my chance of finding a mate is slim unless I try to abduct someone. However, whomever I brought here would probably be very unhappy, as well as not having the physical stamina to live under these conditions.

I know that in the future, loneliness as well as the destruction of the forest will be my enemies. I will need to make some important decisions. Should I attempt to live secretly in the city? Should I take my own life? Why is it important for me to live? I become depressed when I think of these questions.

My great-grandmother had many books from the late 1900s when it seemed there were some people who believed in preserving some aspect of the old way of life; my great-grandmother was one of these. Remember, religion, intuition, mystery and other unscientific thinking are forbidden. These are the kind of books my great-grandmother had stored away. These are the books on which I grew up.

I believe there is a quantum connection between the known and the unknown, between scientific law and creative intuition, between man's domain and God's creation, between the individual human and all living cells in the universe, between the life principle as we see it and the life principle that is.

Even now, the SAC is weakening as people despair, as people suffer the unending boredom of life without purpose. People crave for something other than what the SAC offers. People crave an open-ended system that includes the possibility of life that connects beyond the material.

What about me? Yes, I am lonely and crave companionship. However, I do enjoy a quiet union with animals, sunrays, rainfall, flowers, rocks and the food I eat. The rain forest is a great living macrocosm of what I am. I meditate in silence and the Creator touches me, satisfies me and relieves my loneliness.

I meditate over the food I eat from the forest abundance. The earth sustains my cells. All living cells from the beginning share the gift of life.

I leave my testament to be found and read by you who might chance to come this way. Someday soon I will enter the city and attempt to teach others what I have learned in the rain forest. If I die for this truth, so be it!

Zechariah of Abijah

I am Zechariah of Abijah, husband to Elizabeth, father of John and priest of the Hebraic community of Judah. Once, I was a respected member of the community. I preached in the synagogue and was able, through God's favor, to arouse deep and abiding faith within the people. I had especially enjoyed long, intense discussions of the Torah and how it applied to our life under the Romans. My favor among the people began to fade as my wife and I grew old and childless. Eventually, I myself lost the vision of what was to come. Now, I need to explain how I learned that God's promise blinds us by its mystery.

As Moses led our ancestors to the Promised Land we awaited the new Moses to fulfill God's promise. Our ancestors waited over four hundred years to be delivered from Egyptian slavery, as we now wait for everlasting freedom. Can there have been a more patient people in the history of mankind? However, patience is not without conflict—conflict between the elders who hold the faith and the young who are constantly tempted to abandon it.

Many of our leaders fell in step with the Romans. Some of our people acted more like Romans than Hebrews. Yet, most of us held strongly to the promise that we preached in the synagogue. Some preached with strong emotions and some with the cool reasoning of the Romans. The message was the same: "Have faith, hold on, the signs are around us that the Savior is to come soon." Every young boy was raised as if he were to be the Savior. Meanwhile, those who took up this calling were beheaded, crucified, burned at the stake or simply whipped to death. What other tribe in the history of the world has endured as we?

I am of ninety years now and was approximately sixty years when my world collapsed. First was the shame of being childless, then depression over the relentless persecution of the Romans, then the pregnancy of my wife's unmarried niece and finally the bizarre pretenses of my wife. At sixty years of age Elizabeth told the whole community that she was with child and began preparing for the birth of a baby. This final shame angered me against God—the unfair, unjust, unruly God who allows people to suffer and be led astray. Good people destroyed by God's inaction. I realized that for all these years I inspired people to hope and yet my words could not heal one wound. Over a long time, everyone suffered; many became depressed and most died with unfulfilled dreams. I despaired! At first, I could no longer preach in the synagogue. Eventually, I could not enter into discussions with the other men and finally I could not speak to my wife. To this day, I am not sure whether I could not speak or would not speak. All that I know is that one day with a great feeling of emptiness something snapped and speech failed me.

When my wife's niece, Mary, came to visit, Elizabeth was elated and the two of them, one pregnant without a husband and the other pretending to be pregnant, made newborn clothes and laughed as if everything was right with the world. My silent depression deepened as I failed to see anything good about God's creation, God's promise or God himself. Friendless and Godless, I felt like stone—a silent monolith battered by all the ills of the world into tomb-like submission. Everyone thought I was sick while I with a clear head could only see the sickness of the world around me—a sickness that no words could heal.

Elizabeth ate as if she were eating for two and grew fat as if she were really with child. She was the laughingstock of the community. Our household was possessed by the evil one. No one came near. Everyone avoided us.

Now you might call me simply foolish and that all became right again when Elizabeth proved to be truly with child and gave birth to a perfectly healthy boy whom we called John. Yes, I did feel a little better and thanked God appropriately. I could never again preach in the synagogue or discuss God's intentions. I had lost all confidence that I could understand any of it. Therefore, even though I began to speak again, I spoke as little as possible and then only on factual matters of daily necessities. I remained lost, abandoned by God. God might speak through others, but definitely not through me.

Elizabeth died at seventy when John was merely ten years old, and four years later John ran away from home. He went to the desert to live with some wandering ascetics. He had always been a strange, unruly child, fighting and arguing about everything and everyone. I must say however, he was as tough on himself as he was on others. He would challenge his friends to great feats of endurance and pain. He would always accept the challenge first and if he failed to do the task he would not ask others to try. However, if he was able to do it, he goaded the others and shamed them into trying. I couldn't handle him. He didn't understand why I couldn't stand up in the synagogue and teach the people the strength of the Torah. I thought he was ashamed of me, and I grew more despondent. It was almost a relief when he ran away even though my sadness increased.

Thirty years since John's birth, I am old and about to die. After years of torment I see my son John come out of the desert preaching a version of the Torah never preached before. With fire in his eyes he believes the Savior is with us now. Some say John is a madman; some say he is the Savior. He says that he prepares the way for another.

What do I think? I think I am happy to see my son standing before men and challenging them to the strength of his convictions. I am sad for my own wasted years and if I were young again I would follow my son into the desert.

My son preaches repentance. I wept for my sins and asked God for hope. People had not angered me; I had been angry with God. Once I asked God's forgiveness the anger left me. I am again ready to believe that the Messiah will come.

I will pass away; my generation will pass as generation after generation have passed. Perhaps my son John's generation will see the fulfillment of the promise. Perhaps many more generations will pass before the expected one comes. Perhaps each of us is Messiah in our own way. Regardless, my generation successfully kept the faith.

Wedding Wisdom

(a short dramatic dialogue)

An empty stage except for a Buddhist prayer bench stage right of center and a kneeler left.

A robed Buddhist (Bd, male or female) enters from stage right in walking meditation, stops at the prayer bench, sits and begins to meditate.

A Christian man or woman (Ch) in contemporary dress enters from stage left, quickly walks to the kneeler and begins say aloud the Our Father.

Half way through the Our Father a cherub-type person enters and ties an end of a golden rope around each of them at the waist. They are unaware of being attached with the rope.

Finishing, the Christian, stage left, notices the Buddhist. The Christian turns to the Buddhist and says:

Ch: Excuse me, but what are you doing?

(No answer)

Ch: Excuse me! (A little louder)

(The Bd turns only the head to acknowledge the Ch)

Ch: What are you doing?

Bd: Practicing! (Flatly)

Ch: Practicing what?

Bd: Sitting!

Ch: What is the point of that? (With a little arrogance)

Bd: I sit to become aware of my breath, aware of the moment and aware of the interconnectedness of all things.

Ch: Oh....

(The Ch goes back to praying out loud)

Bd: What are you doing?

Ch: I'm praying!

Bd: What is prayer?

CH: Prayer is...lifting my thoughts to God. (Very pleased to answer)

Bd: Why? (Flatly)

Ch: There are different reasons...to thank God for my life...to ask God's help for others or myself...or maybe to simply praise God.

Bd: Hmm....Can this praying be done silently?

Ch: Yes—Oh! You mean I have been disturbing you. I'm sorry!

(Both return to praying or meditating silently)

Ch: Do you believe in God?

(Bd turns towards Ch yet remains silent)

Ch: You seem to be silent on the subject of God.... Are you uncomfortable? Perhaps we ought to move away from each other.

(Both stand up and begin to move further away, the rope pulls both to the ground, they fall.)

Ch: It seems we are attached. (Both tugging at the rope desperately trying to detach.)

Bd: It seems that way. The earth has shrunk.

Ch: I guess so...trains, planes and automobiles!

Bd: Not to mention satellites, television, radio and intercontinental ballistic missiles.

Ch: You can throw in global warming, lack of ozone, decimation of oxygen-making forests and lack of water and food in some parts of the world.

Bd: I guess we are inter-are?

Ch: Inter what?

Bd: It's a Buddhist principle of the interconnectedness of all beings.

Ch: (still connected) I'm going to turn away so that we do not distract one another.

(Ch begins to pray with his or her back to Bd)

(After a few moments)

Bd: Just because we cannot see one another, are we any less connected? (Pointing out the rope)

(Silence)

Are you uncomfortable because I am silent about God?

Ch: Yes! I bet you're silent on Jesus too.

Bd: On the contrary. Jesus was a manifestation of all that is good. He has all the characteristics of a Buddha...a Bodhisattva! And your Holy Spirit is present in our practice of mindful love and compassion. We give the name of Avalokiteshvara, the Buddha of Compassion, to our ideal of love and compassion, a feminine quality you idealize in the Blessed Virgin.

Ch: We have some things in common: but if you do not accept Jesus as the Son of God who saved us from our sins we have little to talk about when it comes to religion. We may coexist (noting the rope) but we don't have to talk!

Bd: On the contrary, we have much more to share. I simply don't speak of God because I have no words that satisfy the totality of being and the single nature of all that is. For me, God is more of a state of being. Jesus is the son of God, so is Buddha and so are we all sons and daughters of God.... That is my practice. The Buddha taught that life is full of sorrow and pain. Silent breathing and chanting connects me to the moment and to all of creation. I practice so that I can be sensitive and loving wherever I am and with whomever I am present...even my enemy.

Ch: Yes! Jesus said we should love our enemies.... I'm confused...I simply know what I practice. I practice Christianity and believe in a personal God and you do not.

Bd: That may be so. But the fact remains that we remain connected and there is nothing we can do about it. It is words that separate us. It is our incomplete thoughts and ideas. Basically, we see things as we were conditioned to see them by the people around us.

Ch: Christ said that we should be like little children. Maybe that explains how we were all the same as children and grew apart as a result of our conditioning.

Bd: Buddhists believe that we should not grasp or hold onto anything. We should surrender all notions. This allows us to love under any circumstances.

Ch: Christ also said one must leave everything behind to take up the cross and follow him. Perhaps, he was referring to our notions of things as well as the things themselves. He said we shouldn't judge or we'll be judged, that we shouldn't look for the splinter in our neighbor's eye when we have a log in our own.

Bd: How would you characterize the path Christ wants you to follow?

Ch: Let me think.... Ah...yes, The Beatitudes:

> Happy are the poor in spirit; theirs is the kingdom of heaven.
> Happy are the gentle; they shall inherit the earth.
> Happy are those who mourn; they shall be comforted.
> Happy are those who hunger and thirst for what is right; they shall
> be satisfied.
> Happy are the merciful; they shall have mercy shown them.
> Happy are the pure in heart; they shall see God.

Happy are the peacemakers; they shall be called children of God.

Happy are those who are persecuted in the cause of right; theirs is the
kingdom of heaven.

Bd: That is great! I like that. Those Beatitudes fit in beautifully with everything I believe. I could use them as a mindfulness chant (begins to chant the Beatitudes)....

Ch: Wait a minute...I have an idea.... Simply cherish all that is, all beings, and you will be united with God's nature. Under these circumstances no man-made corporate body, political border, organizational rules or distinctions apply.

Bd: If you live with the enlightenment of the Buddha, you live with Jesus.

Ch: If you identify with Jesus you live in the enlightenment of the Buddha.

Bd: If you seek this path no divisions exist, and each of us can follow the practices that help us to achieve the way of loving-kindness.

Ch: Then I can be Christian, attend my Christian church, put my faith in Jesus and study the Bible.

Bd: I can be Buddhist, attend my Sangha, put my faith in Buddha and study the Dharma.

Ch: Perhaps we can learn from one another how to improve our practice.

Bd: If we follow the path of love, our differences will not fall into a cacophony of argument, dispute and war.

Ch: A marriage of wisdom traditions where each can maintain their individuality.

Bd: Unity amidst diversity.

Ch: Our love can prevent chaos in the world.

(The two wind themselves up in the golden rope and walk out arm in arm.)

The Unforgiving Sea and the Forgiving God

(A monologue)

This is a true story, or at least based on a true incident. I was a young officer of the U.S. Coast Guard stationed in San Francisco with Coast Guard District 12—Command Western area. My office was on the 17th floor of a building in the business district that overlooked San Francisco Bay. I lived across the bay in Oakland and drove the Oakland Bay Bridge to work daily. I parked near the shipping wharf and its warehouses. Even though it was a hike to the office, the parking there was free.

One night I worked very late. It was dark and the fog had rolled in. While I walked to my car, suddenly a large figure of a man in a black overcoat stepped from the shadows. One of his eyes was half-closed and a great dark bulbous growth consumed his cheek beneath it.

"Hey, mate! Can you spare me 50 cents for a cup of coffee? Say, you're a naval officer, aren't you? I sailed that unforgiving sea for over 30 years. I've been on ships that sunk during WWII, three to be exact. I saw men die; I saved a few. Yeah, an unforgiving sea and a forgiving God. I bet you're not married. I was married a few times; don't know where those wives are now. It's not easy to be married when you're in the Merchant Marine."

"Let me give you some advice...before you marry a woman, give her a good shower bath. These days you don't have any idea what a woman looks like till you give her a good shower bath. I met a woman once in a bar. We got along real good. I went to her apartment with her. In the middle of the night I woke up and leaned over to give her a little hug...she was bald! She didn't look like the same woman at all. That's why I say you give the woman a good shower bath before you get serious."

"I may be ugly but I'm not dumb. I read the newspaper every day. As I'm reading, I hold a pencil in my hand; when I read something I know to be true, I mark a little number two in the column. I keep on reading; when I see something else I know to be true, I mark another little two. When I come to the conclusion, I know it's right because 2 and 2 equals 4."

"Hey, how about that 50 cents? No, I don't want a dollar...50 cents will get me that cup of coffee...you don't have any change? All right, I'll take the dollar...but...I owe you 50 cents. See you mate.... May your sails be full and the sea calm. Now, that would be a miracle by the unforgiving sea and the forgiving God."

Understanding Monsters

A modern dramatization combining two ancient stories

(The drum sounds and sounds, picking up its heartbeat-like pace until it is into a state of panic.

As the drumbeat picks up a boy enters from the rear running up and down the aisle, crouching, shuddering and looking extremely panicked and frightened. He approaches people in the audience asking them if the monster is there)

Where is it? Is the monster here? Have you seen the monster? Run for your lives, the monster is coming. Where is it? Is it here? Where is the monster? Is he coming?

(Now the boy is crouching at the front, hysterically frightened of something ...nothing happens...time passes and he begins to calm down. He stands up. The drum beat slows and then stops)

I'm tired of running scared. I do not want to be scared any longer. Ah ha.... *(Discovering a large stick)*

I'll use this to protect myself and need not be afraid any longer. If that monster comes, I'll hit him with this...I'll hit him...I'll hit him...I'll hit him!! *(Wildly swinging the stick)* I don't need to be scared of anything any longer. Anybody gets in my way, I'll show them with this stick who's boss.... Hey, kid...what are you looking at? You'd better not look at me like that or I'll hit you one.... Get out of my way. Can't you see who I am? I'm not afraid of anything....

(The scared boy is now a monster strutting around the stage bullying imaginary people) I'm hungry! Give me that food.... Move away! I want this space.... *(Walking quickly drawing a very large circle, he threatens everyone with his stick)* Listen all of you, I'm the boss! Can you hear me? I'm the boss! I'm the boss!

(An elderly man or woman enters the stage not even noticing the young boy monster. He's wandering around as if admiring the scenery. He might even be talking to himself about the beauty he is seeing)

The boy: Hey you! What are you doing?

(The old man continues as if not hearing the boy)

Can't you hear me? I'm the boss and I want you to come here. Come here!

(The old man continues to ignore the boy...the boy goes to the old man, grabs him and forces him to face him)

Old man: Yes, did you want something of me?

Boy: Do you know who I am? I am he who could beat you with my club until dead. For you, I am death!

Old man: Do you know who I am? I am he who would allow you to beat me to death and think nothing of it. For you, I am eternal life!

Boy: *(laughing)* Old man, you pretend to be wise and holy. You ought to know about heaven and hell. Describe them to me. Tell me all you know about heaven and hell and if I don't like what you say, I'm going to beat you.

Old man: I can't.

Boy: And why not!

Old man: Because you are much too stupid.

Boy: What did you say? (Enraged)

Old man: Besides that, you are much too ugly!

Boy: Aaghhhh.... I'll beat you for that!

Old man: Now, that is hell.

(Struck by the wisdom of the old man's words, the boy drops the stick, kneels down and says)

Boy: I'm sorry...please...please forgive me.

Old man: Now, that is heaven.

(The old man helps the boy to his feet, puts his arm around him and speaks to him as they walk out down the center aisle)

Old man: You see, monsters are driven by fears, fear of being hurt or fear of having something taken away. Anyone can become a monster if they allow the bad things that happen to them turn them into one. When you see people hurting others, of course you want to stop them. You also must feel sorry for them because inside they are simply scared and hurt people....

Narrator: The Holy Man was not scared of the boy and his stick. He had long ago conquered the monster within himself. Therefore, whatever threat was put on him; he did not react out of fear or anger. The Holy Man understands why people become monsters, why they do harmful things to one another, why they war, why they want to execute criminals. He also understands the criminals and the reasons why they become who they are. The Holy Man understands God's message to love one another, even our enemies.

School Wall

(a monologue)

(Lights fade, spotlight shifts to sleeping wall; the wall stirs, it stretches, yawns, opens its eyes, looks around and finally notices the audience)

Oh, Hi...I'm a wall...a particular wall...I'm part of this building...I'm an old wall, but I'm young in spirit. I even have a new coat of paint...you know something, people ought to pay more attention to walls because walls contain you. Oh...no...I didn't mean that! Who likes to be contained? Tuna fish is contained in cans and people aren't tuna fish. I guess what I'm trying to say is that a wall is like a mother. No, that won't do either. I mean we shelter you, we house you, and we always try to leave a door open. That's getting too deep....

I'll tell you what. I'll tell you why I like being a wall, especially here. When I came here—years ago—this place was exciting and fun. I mean, any wall likes to be part of a new building, but an amazing thing happened; that excitement never left me. So here I am—years later, happy to be a wall. Being old but freshly painted gives me a kind of maturity that doesn't leave my fun times behind. If it's possible, you might say that I'm old and young at the same time....

Besides being old and young at the same time, there is another interesting thing about me.... I've learned a lot about myself here. In math and science I learned how I'm constructed and how my brothers and I hold up this whole building. In social studies, I learned about all the other walls all over the world. The walls over which battles were fought; the walls within which great treaties were signed; the walls behind which lovers hide.

The walls I like to learn most about though are the walls of the future. You know, the kind that house those spacemen, those spacemen in their little cabins circling the earth. When the teachers talk about all the new materials that walls will be made of, I really get excited.... Oh, oh.... The next class is coming in; I'd better be quiet and pay attention.